SUZANNE AND THE PACIFIC

SUZANNE
AND THE PACIFIC

BY

JEAN GIRAUDOUX

TRANSLATED BY

BEN RAY REDMAN

❧

NEW YORK

Howard Fertig

1975

Originally published in French as Suzanne et le Pacifique
First published in English in 1923
Copyright, 1923, by Jean Giraudoux
Copyright 1939 Editions Bernard Grasset
Howard Fertig, Inc. Edition 1975
Published by arrangement with Editions
Grasset et Fasquelle
All rights reserved.

Library of Congress Cataloging in Publication Data
Giraudoux, Jean, 1882-1944.
    Suzanne and the Pacific.
    Translation of Suzanne et le Pacifique.
    Reprint of the ed. published by Putnam, New York.
    I.   Title.
PZ3.G442Su10 [PQ2613.I74]   843'.9'12   75-5831

Printed in the United States of America

SUZANNE
AND THE PACIFIC

BY

JEAN GIRAUDOUX

TRANSLATED BY

BEN RAY REDMAN

&

G. P. Putnam's Sons
New York & London
The Knickerbocker Press
1923

Facsimile of the title page of the original edition.

Suzanne and the Pacific

CHAPTER I

IT was one of those days when nothing happens;
when the stars, who are accustomed to variety,
feeling that life will be monotonous until evening,
go out without employment and huddle together like
chickens when the rain is going to last. There was
a bit of everything in the sky. There was the sun;
there was the moon, under a cover. Night and
morning were both served on the same shining
cloths. The south wind fell perpendicularly upon the
east wind, and the north-west-south-east breezes
caressed one in the right angle. The bells were
ringing: when the knocker struck their eastern side,
already warm, the sound was half again more tender.
Everyone was at his door, giving his shadow to the
sun. The postman zigzagged from one sidewalk
to the other; he seemed drunk with fine weather; the
street was not broad enough. He scarcely hurried;
he observed the opening of each envelope, and saw

each piece of news pass from secrecy to blinding day. Then he made me one of those signs with his arm which have been forbidden in the postal service since Morse, and held toward me a letter on which I saw the Australian stamp . . .

I blushed . . .

For I always blush when a foreign country is mentioned . . .

I was eighteen years old. I was happy. I lived with my tutor in a house that was all length, in which every *porte-fenêtre* opened on the town, every window on a countryside of hills and streams, with fields and chestnut groves like patches . . . , for it was a land which had already seen much service, —it was Limousin. On market days I had only to turn in my chair in order to shut out the market and to rediscover the country, empty of its flocks. It was my habit to make this half-turn on all occasions, seeking for each passerby—for the priest and the sub-prefect—his counterweight of emptiness and silence among the hills. And changing the kingdom of sounds was scarcely more difficult: I had only to change windows. On the street side: children playing train, a phonograph, the trumpeting of news-papers, and the ducks and kids being carried to the kitchens, uttering cries which became more and more metallic as they approached their death cries. On the mountain side: the real train, and the bellowings and bleatings which one could anticipate in winter from the vapor around the muzzles of the animals. There we dined in summer, on a terrace. Sometimes it was the week when the acacias perfumed the air, and we ate them in the fritters; or the larks riddled the sky, and we ate them in the patés. Or it was the day when the rye becomes pure gold and has its unique day of triumph over the wheat: we ate pancakes of rye. A gun-shot in a coppice: the woodcock were passing, going in a day to Central Africa, explained my tutor in order to make me blush. A shepherd girl striking her wooden shoes against each other: twenty years ago that was the summons against wolves, now it served against foxes, in another twenty years it would be used only against martins. Then the sun set, aslant, wishing to wound my old country only in seton. One saw it halved for a moment, sheltered by the hill, like an actor. Applause would have been enough to make it return. But all remained silent . . . Illumined from behind, all the branches and the slightest twigs seemed to lift themselves, all the trees abandoned themselves . . . One wished to reassure them . . .

Despite one's self, one made a half-gesture to reassure them . . . A great bird flew very high, the
only thing still lighted in this lowly world: one was
moved at seeing him, as though there were among
birds no species which flew high but only a
solitary and ever-shining sparrow-hawk . . . At
a distance a poacher was fishing for crawfish, and his
lantern followed the stream. The wind arose, turning back the leaves of our prisoner oaks and alders,
giving them all the color of willows. One smiled
at following this fire which was teasing the water,
this air which was teasing the earth; the four elements, sleepy, and gently at play. As a premium we
abandoned our faces to the first star; we withdrew a
little at the second. From the Montagne de Blond a
hululu arose: It was the Grand Duke of the Cévennes,
said my tutor, the greatest after the Grand Duke of
the Andes. A round, round moon, from which all
clouds had been thrust away, which seemed at times
to turn backward, as if it were going to veer about
what Mademoiselle every evening called the car of
night; a moon which, had it been compared to that
of Batavia, would have sufficed to make me and all
like me weep, rose . . . Marie could be heard in
the room on her last visit, turning down the beds.
Suddenly, the gas flared up in the street, and the car

of night really turned, chasing the bats . . . It was then that the bell rang and my friends arrived.

I am going to tell you their height, their color.— By pushing all three of them in front of me, I can, perhaps, at last begin this story. I am going to tell you the length of their hair, their size. As soon as I place a white sheet of paper in front of me, two dissimilar persons take flight, like our shadows under a gas jet; but of myself nothing remains. I have so long been compelled, in an unparalled seclusion and solitude, by necessity or by play, to let my heart, my will, even my body dominate and frighten me at times, like those of a creature infinitely bigger and stronger than myself, or, on the contrary, time and again, to repress the gestures of a child in arms, to recover painfully in my inward depths all that is minutest like thought, most vegetable like soul, that I find myself accustomed to choose when I wish to recount my adventure, only between a gigantic and a microscopic image of myself. Like all women writers, I have tried my best to place myself so as to feel neither too strange nor too familiar toward myself when confronted by my mirror. I have tried my best to make myself write a first phrase, a first memory, seized at random. It is finished: this intractable person that is in me abandons me

when I tug on her, on her hand or her entire arm, and my phrase remains alone. But today,
in order to tame her, I am going to march my
little band of friends in front of her; and if I speak
of myself immediately after describing them, you
may perhaps perceive at its true height—two
centimeters less than Juliette, two sizes larger than
Victoria—a soul which, in the following chapters,
I shall try neither to enlarge nor to contract.

Victoria had a seventeen ankle and a thirty calf.
She and I were born on the same day. Our life for
eighteen years was a kind of little game, which each
struggled to win by arriving a second earlier at table
or ten centimeters ahead in the garden. But I could
beat her only at running. She could see smoke and
birds while to all the rest of us they still remained
invisible. As to memories, she had some which went
back to her first year, and which astonished her parents. At night, she could identify the village of a
peasant from his step, which she found differed
according to the community. A very few beings
with senses as acute would have served to populate
France exactly, so that everything, even the work
of wrens and moles, would be under a human control.
Then, too, when she wished you a happy birthday,
you had the impression of being at the exact anniver-

sary, to the minute, of your birth. When she said, "You are right," one experienced in effect, that little illumination, that sense of well-being, which is reason coming undone within one. On her each object, each feature, assumed its value and its mission: her eyebrows were firm, and, when it rained, kept the water from rolling down her forehead into her eyes, and, since they met, her nose was also sheltered. Her eyelashes successfully protected her eyes from dust and fitted together like a large-toothed comb when a sliver of straw lodged in them. Her hair was long, so as to clothe her, and golden chestnut, so as to render her invisible once clothed. Her forefinger vacillated constantly like a compass needle; and when one saw her in wait for a hare, crouched down ready to leap, one understood why the knees of men and women bend inward and not outward.

Juliette Lartigue was even more alive, but less purposefully. Her eyes shone when she was hungry. Her mouth watered at the purchase of perfumes, and her nose quivered at mention of God. She disposed of a host of reflexes, all false. She distributed boxes on the ear during holy week; she held out her hand to discover whether it was fine weather; and when one of her eyelashes glided over her cheek she captured and crunched it. The sight of one animal always tore from her the cry of a different animal; and when one heard her sing one felt easy; it meant that she was sleepy. Sometimes she made up meticulously: that meant we were going to the pool to bathe. She would speak in twin, contradictory phrases, beginning the one by the word "physically," and the other by "morally."

"Physically," she would say, "he is very bad; morally he is perfect. Sensually she is serious; morally she is light."

In regard to herself, also, she had made this distinction from childhood. Deep reflection during a period of quarantine had thus cut her in two at the age of nine, and we had acquired the habit of calling her by her first name or by her family name according to whether it was the physical Juliette or her ethereal opposite which was in question. She never made a mistake in this matter:

"What are you thinking, Juliette?"

Juliette thought that her skin, while she rubbed it, felt like death.

"Hola! Lartigue, what are you thinking?"

For we would surprise her to make her come out of her part. But Lartigue in the midst of this agitation, and even under our combined weights—for we had jumped on her—thought definitely that the soul is immortal.

As a result, we used to send in her direction everything that seemed to us especially physical,—crabs, crawfish, spiders,—or everything outside our ethics, —incest, murder, taoism,—leaving to her the task of testing the frontiers of our souls. So she passed prettily, once or twice a minute, from nothingness to perfect grace. I forgot to say that her left hand was always cold, her right hand warm . . . Of all of us, she, in sum, weighed the least; but it was she, however, whom we would call quickly in the face of each emotion, each sunset, as one puts a gramme in one scale in order to balance an envelope in the other.

Marie-Sévère is dead now. She was condemned; we had been forewarned of her sudden death. For ten years our eyes watched over her without relaxation; and one cannot exaggerate the number of times that a slight quivering or glittering on the face of a friend makes one swear that it is the precursor of death. Each of her desires was for us her last desire; it was authoritative and we hastened to obey it. Sometimes she seemed to yield to us, but in the end she would reassert her own will . . .

"You must not have any more ice, Marie-Sévère."

"No. I must not . . . I want some . . ."

As soon as our boarding-school conversation became expansive; when we spoke of country, of secret marriages, of Chinese tortures, she was silent and uncomfortable, as if she had had an intolerable experience of all these things. She died in my home, in my room; and I, all that week, slept in her home, in her bed, finding on awakening all her clothes, her furniture, her soap, sad at the feeling that I was inhabiting her very body. Juliette and Victoria shunned me; I carried her perfume. She died slowly, surely, consumed like those individuals who martyrize themselves by bearing on their persons a capsule of radium. And of her, always idle and egotistic, there remains to us the same memory as though she had been devoted to a great cause. She wished to be preferred to each of us, and she allowed each of us to believe herself her favorite. We were gathered around her on the day of her death:

"It is happy to die," she said simply, "before the person one loves!"

Her avoidance of the plural was unmistakable.

"You are not dying, Marie-Sévère!"

"No, I'm not dying . . . I am dying."

Our cousins and our teachers taught us life. They taught us to call walks "rounds"; death, "the comrade"; and to use as often as possible the expression *grace d'état*. Perhaps they gave us a false notion of the world. I wish to cite only what we were sure of, and of which we had checked the evidence. We learned that in America the prostitutes steal from men and remain pure, but that they are, in fact, thieves. In France, on the contrary, the female thieves prefer to steal among themselves, for they become amorous of their chloroformed victims. They taught us that in their lichen-covered Sweden the Swedish women are volcanos of snow and fires of ice. That the Little-Russian women imitate the handwriting of twenty different men whom they desire, address to themselves twenty proposals of marriage, refuse them by twenty motivated replies, and go scornfully through the world. That American men—like their students who come to Paris only to learn architecture—come to copy in the hearts of Frenchwomen I know not what architecture of happiness, thereafter departing at a gallop to build in Minneapolis in the breasts of giant young girls almost always named Watson. They left us in no ignorance regarding Turkestan, where the Sultan, enemy of caterpillars and garden lice, is preceded in

his garden by three little girls who crush these insects between their fingers; or of the Shah of Persia,
who during his stay in Paris sold Persia to England,
and who—under the name of M. Teheran—wished
in exchange to steal the most beautiful dancer at the
Opera from M. Sanchez y Toledo. My tutor read
to us from *Debats* (irritated by our whispering) the
news from Arabia where women marry at the age
of ten,—(were we going to shut up?)—where they
are deformed at seventeen, one word, one word,
and we would be old women! Or of Monte Carlo,
where the Duchess Coupeau used far-sighted glasses
to place her stake, then near-sighted ones to follow
the ball, which could be seen turning brilliantly so
far off that it was, *grâce d'état,* in the eye of the
Princess Kohn. They taught us that in the subway
in Paris, a well-behaved woman may smile at the
young man opposite with her reflection in the window
—always clear because of the tunnel; with her reflection only, being severe and disdainful when she
looks at him directly. And, with all our reflections,
we did not miss any chance of smiling or making
promises for the future, promises of marriage;
while we were bashful and unrelenting when we
looked straight ahead. Slightly Oriental, we fought
over a square of *rahat loucoum,* as one fights over

a dry cake, each one of us pulling it toward her.
Sometimes old generals, affecting a perfect paternal-
ism, took us by the waist and pulled at our tresses,
shaking our heads without succeeding in shaking our
eyes, which we made as implacable as two disks. We
had a piano teacher who was incompetent but good
hearted; so, by stealth, we had a Professor
of the Conservatory come from Limoges. We had
an old confessor who was deaf; so we went once a
month for supplementary confession to the canon of
Saint-Martial. But both our piano teacher and our
confessor were pleased with us—our progress on
the piano and in wisdom disconcerting Bellac—and
delighted with themselves. We had unruly cousins,
pimply and plowed up by youthful razors; but
every Friday, at Limoges, we were followed by unknown Hussar lieutenants, the delightful cousins of
other girls. As a result life, and the soul already
appeared double to us. All those things which later
were to become our weapons penetrated to us through
the most secret channels: Baume Salva in a dummy
book, Beauty Cream hidden in gingerbread, the rice
powder of the Emperor of China in the pocket of a
muff; like the instruments which, once collected, can
be used to saw through a prisoner's bars. Then we
smeared our cheeks with these secret things, we

displayed them on our faces, and marched them innocently along the Promenade de Coq. Our hair stuffed with invisible golden pins, one of which would sometimes fall to the ground without our deigning to notice it; we would leave it to be gathered up by a duenna, treating it as a Queen treats a clumsy lover. Red and black ribbons came suddenly from our sleeves; and if these had been pulled, we might perhaps have opened up like boxes of sugarplums. We had pyjamas which we put on at midnight; we awakened before dawn in order to replace these by our night-gowns, and no one ever surprised us in our metamorphoses. We had discovered, after fifteen years of spying and experience, that it is between three-twenty and four-ten that the weariness of life makes itself felt in our elders, and their vigilance is relaxed. After three-twenty-one, we inhaled a vial of ether, we smoked an amber colored cigarette, we opened a bottle of Celestins to determine if it really is the water which tastes most like tears, we burned holly over a candle in order to get the exact smell of opium,—and, when the most suspicious of the tired creatures arrived at four-eleven, he found only two open windows, two open doors, and a witch-like perfume . . .

Thus, every afternoon, all four of us pooled our

few years, and the one who had the right to take
more than her share became our guardian; the other,
who could take less than her share, our child. We
felt ourselves an entire body, whose senses were
scarcely scratched, which demons could no more
penetrate than rain can get into an ear. It would
have been easy for us—with Victoria who, by her
memory, was so close to a former existence, and with
Marie-Sévère who was so neighborly to death—to
have made of our present years a realm more re-
stricted and more pathetic than that platform on
which Norwegian and Russian girls box with life.
But we were French girls. At Bellac one let oneself
be conducted by hunger and thirst, by weariness and
sleep—the only tides in the country—and by everything which spreads out or gathers a family around
its house or farm. The strap which unites the two
meals and the curtain which is drawn at evening
both functioned perfectly. Unlike Parisian snobs,
we did not seek destiny or politics in the words of
porters. Nor did we cheat in anecdotes in order to
give the world an appearance of folly or stupidity.
We did not meet Kipling's cousin the day that we
pronounced his name; our coffin-maker was not
named Courteline. We had eyes which were not
false-bottomed, and oval hearts which were never on

2

the bias; and all those people who appear as strange creatures to Parisians—Russian grand-dukes who breakfast while playing the drum, American women who shave their heads in order to wear wigs of tulle—we pitied, seeing that theirs was a bad business. Nor was there talk of divine malediction descending on our cousins or our parents; and when they went out to hunt we were sure that if there were two partridges, one marked by God, the other an ordinary one, their gun would turn irresistibly toward the younger.

Our town was located on the national highway which runs from Paris to Toulouse, our furthest domains extending some leagues to the south; and between milestone 405 and milestone 420—reaching the highest number when it was continued fine weather—we tasted, as it is also called at Bellac, life in its fullness. Whenever we returned from the gardens, our baskets were so overflowing that it was possible to follow our track by the black-currant bushes, the raspberry bushes, and the strawberry beds; and those of the dogs who liked fruit better than worms preferred following us to following the plows. At night we could hear through the open window falls which were soft or hard according to the season: it was the apricots or the nuts which were falling. In summer our parents sometimes slept away from home and after dinner we returned home alone. At first reasonably, along the sand-stone road on which our heels sounded; then through the meadows, shoes in hand; then, our feet bare at last, along the stream itself. We went at night without leaving a trace. The sun, on a level with the black and red buckwheat fields, was still large enough to hold one of our heads, or the whole body of one of us who was a little way off. We played at hiding ourselves, forgetting to designate the searcher, and each of us remained stretched out, without saying a word, without a move, soon unconscious of herself. The first quail recalled us—bird signals were already useful to us—and we set off again. It was night. The praise of fine weather passed suddenly from crickets to toads. An old peasant greeted us, and received in return four clear salutations. Juliette leaned on my arm before the shadow, if it was not Lartigue before the unknown leaning upon my silence. Victoria saw the first owl; at the instant when we finally perceived it, she heard its flight; when we heard it, she smelled its antlike odor which was for us a mystery. And the clay from the quarries glided softly like the sand in an hour-glass.

Life!

What is there that life does not promise, when from a hilltop, at an equal distance from sleeping parents and grandparents, one suddenly perceives the electric lights of Bellac, all lighted like the thousand bulbs in a telephone office, all insisting that one speak to them, shooting and importunate. Bells also called to us—an old system—from all the folds in the plain and mountain where men know best how to rest and sleep. Every poplar shivered, every stream flowed, every belated dove offered itself and expanded within us like a metaphor. It was the one moment when we dared, through the night as through black glasses with which one can outstare the sun, to look directly at our destiny, our happiness; and all those little fires below and all those little fires above seemed only sparks.

We leaned our elbows on the railing of the summerhouse. We were silent. Sometimes there was a cracking sound in an orchard: the overloaded branch of a plum tree had broken, a hundred young fruits were condemned to death. Or there was a cry from a furrow: the shrew-mouse had been seized by the brown owl. A star shot. All these caresses of early death, or of an ancient and outworn death, pleased our hearts and gave them a momentary sense of immortality . . . Behind us the whole past of the

world was suddenly piled up, and we buttressed ourselves against the balustrade to hold it back,—a
feeble barrier. In our slightest glance was held all
that the being can distill from human adventures.
In us stirred all the germs of our future lives, all
probable, all contradictory, all desirable: there was
our near, immediate death, but entwined with our
distant death, with our eternity; our hearts which
were always calm, and our hearts which were always
troubled, the one beside the other, overlapping like
the faces of royal couples on medals; our husbands,
our lovers playing calmly with our fierce jealousy,
our blind confidence; those voyages to Borneo, those
delicious tempests, those beautiful shipwrecks, but
with them that happy, immovable stay in Bellac
where we were born; that dark and beloved for-
eigner, whom we implacably commanded, but with
him that fair Frenchman who was a bit of a grum-
bler, in a big cutaway, near whom we lived passionately, in a false fear; and those avowals in the middle
of a drawing-room to one who did not wish to comprehend; and that flight before the one who pursued
us; and that decision to abandon oneself to everyone,
—to no one; and that thirst for modesty, for self
effacement; and all those millions, and those orgies,
and those honors . . . all these things stirred in us

from the height of scarcely one year's memories. Leaning upon one another we raised ourselves up to breathe the night; we let ourselves be suckled by a sweet black monster, with mouths open but mute, with eyes dilated but unillumined. And Marie-Sévère's large diamond was our only response—a worthy one moreover, it had come from Tobolsk—to so much darkness and to so much light.

A fox which was eating berries from a juniper tree frightened us, and we descended toward the town with big man-like strides. We were reassured at sight of the little fox who was eating. The gaillardes, dahlias, sun-flowers, and cocks-combs which were piled up around each house seemed to have been thrust out of doors in order to purify the air of the sleeper within. The full moon, with a cloud over the spot where we sometimes saw its eyes, assumed the secrecy of a masked moon. We skirted the cemetery, bare and luminous, in one corner of which were standing the shovels, pick-axes and wheelbarrows of the grave-diggers, while in another corner stood a group of three cypress trees,—spindles of the Fates of Bellac, fanned by midnight winds. The heliotrope smelled sweet, standing bolt upright, disdainful of the moon, convinced that by day as by night it gave obedience only to itself. At the first street corner our bodies, already penetrated by so much light, passed under an electric lamp which seemed suddenly to illumine our very souls. Then we came to the houses of friends, in which we knew the location of each bed and sleeper, and we scratched on the shutter when we knew that a head was close at hand. One by one my companions abandoned me, like doubles touched successively by the midnight wind: I hurriedly ascended to my room, pursued closely by some unknown metamorphosis. The trees shivered. It was indeed midnight. Outside could be heard the clashing of a great leaf as it turned. I pronounced my name aloud in order to initial the fresh page; my first name, and then my last name which, for young girls, is more fragile than a first name. All that nocturnal toilet which one makes before a mirror I accomplished in front of a glass without seeing myself; teeth clenched in agony because they held a pin, head bent tenderly in order not to tangle loosened hair. I left the curtains open. I fell asleep with little isolated cold patches on my face and arms where the moon struck me; and suddenly the same spots were warm. I opened my eyes; I had slept eight hours; it was the sun!

Then,—and my story seems never to finish, and

in fact it never did finish,—then we flirted with the mediocre life of the town as with a young cousin. During the day, we were far from that strange life to which we were secretly pledged; affecting a contempt for it, for Verlaine and for Loti, replacing in the daytime the silk word of our nocturnal language by the cotton word, the emerald word by the amethyst word. Small towns are mirrors which do not distort. The virtues and activities of the universe as reflected in Bellac were so regular and so obvious that they were inoffensive. January there was always cold; August, always torrid. At any given time each inhabitant had only one virtue or one vice, and we necessarily learned to know the world in terms of separate seasons and sentiments. Each well-plastered house along the street was a note of avarice, of vanity, or of gluttony. There were no sharps, no flats; no miser-glutton, no modest-egotist. Insensibly we struck with all our might on each, or amused ourselves—as on the day when we had the piano piece which calls for crossed hands —by alternate visits; going from the miser to the prodigal, from the envious man to the contented one. . . .

It was the 14th of July, with flags at the windows in the morning, making a noise at once like that of rain and of fire, with the merry-go-round turning around the liberty tree . . . It was market day, and sleep was troubled by bellowings and neighings which were cut short as if a peasant had stuffed his hand into the mouth of the horse or bull; by stampings, —the monthly march which animals make toward work and death. It was August 15th, Saint-Hortense's day, swollen with sunshine and as noisy as a dissenters' chapel. It was Madam Parpon's death; and her husband, who whistled incessantly, started a mechanical whistle every other minute, checking himself at the first note, with the result that he went about during the first week of mourning making the same noise that a toad does at evening . . . It was a bankruptcy; the lawyer had failed, who the day before had kicked aside my dog while he was lying on the sidewalk, bending over as if to caress him and then crippling him. It was a fire, devouring the hall of the hotel: one could see the glass balls reflect the flames for a moment and then fly into shivers, and the potted plants suddenly reduced to dust, deceived to the last by such a climate. But we approached all these things—the ruin, the national holiday, and the fire itself—without suffering from them; wearing masks of rose mica which the two old generals sometimes touched with their forefingers while wagging their heads. The brother of the King of Portugal passed through Limousin in a coach drawn by twelve mules. He weighed two hundred kilos, while his companion, the Duke of Palmella, weighed a hundred and thirty; but we were not disillusioned. Our future began still beyond that kingdom of which present kings are the extreme marks. We went on our way. The parents of the Merle boy obliged us to feel his eyelashes which he had just cut with a pair of scissors: they were like two tooth-brushes. Jacques Lartigue slipped us the verses which the little librarian poet untiringly dedicated to us, little rhymeless, bent over verses,* in which he changed only the adjectives for each of us, as though he were fishing for trout. From his window where he read the *Odyssey,* attributed to Homer (for he always contested the existence of authors) and *Adolphe,* attributed to Constant, M. de Lardois—after convincing himself that he had proved to us the immortality of the soul by final causes—smiled at our mortal dress and sent us a thousand signs dictated by friendship, the final cause of love. At the edge of the terrace we would find Madame Blébé, covered with powder, with her bare arms painted,

* Play on words: *vers* in French means both verses and worms.

stretched out in the sun, soft and feeble like bread before it has been baked. The two doctors crossed each other: the young one was called in for the aged, the old one was summoned for the young, and neither ever had a patient his own age . . . M. de Lalautie, who had sworn to spend no more money on matches, would stride across the street holding a flaming paper, which he had just thrust into the Dutch-oven of his sister who lived opposite him, in order to light his gas. Winter came, and one fine morning the brown earth was pricked with white points like a plover's egg. Autumn came, and with it the brown furrows which the peasants, loving the earth, effaced with harrows, and the vineyards which they massaged by hand. Summer; Spring. We went on our way, sometimes shedding unfeeling tears; at times burning our hearts with red irons which were quite cold; and our suffering was confined to the two places, small indeed, by which we touched the earth; our feet were a little weary in July; our feet were thoroughly frozen in December.

Well, on this particular day the postman really brought me a letter from Australia. I had won the trip around the world which had been offered as first prize by the *Sydney Daily* in its competition for the best maxim on boredom. "If a man is bored," I had written to Sydney, "stir him up: if a woman is bored hold her fast." In exchange for this advice which was so useful to her, Australia called me, and despite my tutor I departed. Mademoiselle accompanied me. I left Bellac by a night train; if I had left my gas burning, like Phileas Fogg, I could have seen it from the station. Perhaps a trip to a single country would have saddened my friends; but they felt that each step which I took away from them brought me back again; and when the car stopped they pushed me, they hoisted me up without too much weeping, as if they were simply lifting me to a height where the speed of the earth no longer mattered, and were coming back again the next day at the same hour, desirous of news, to catch me on the fly and pull me down in mid-flight.

CHAPTER II

ONCE past Saint Ursin's Chapel, the terminus of her longest journey, everything that Mademoiselle saw was new to her. She could feel in the railway car, as in a peasant's cart, the slightest ascent or descent. She found in the poplars of Vierzon and the porters of Aubrais those striking peculiarities which other explorers no longer perceive save in baobabs and Burmese mules. She leaned over the viaduct at Orleans in order to see her reflection in the water. The women of Étampes detested corsets; their throats were beautiful. The men of Juvisy saluted every time they spoke and wore hats that were too small. She wanted to land at each station as at a port. She was full of solicitude, too, for the travelers who entered or left the train, helping them with their valises, protecting them from the sun, offering them milk and water; as if all these creatures, young and old, were not only new to her but had just been born.

She wished to stay a month in Paris, for all her possessions which were shaky or fragile—two or three teeth, and a pin which closed badly—she had solidly fastened by specialists in anticipation of tempests. Foreseeing typhoons, she procured for herself reënforced glasses. Every morning we left our hotel on the Boulevard Raspail together, and did not return until evening, so between us we cost the doorman only two greetings a day. We would cross the Seine by the great bridge on which the tollgate is opened by a blind man—supreme courtesy of Paris—throwing a glance to the right at Notre-Dame and royalty, and a glance to the left at the Trocadero and the Republic. Going toward the Concorde, we skirted the balustrade of the Tuilleries, bordering the garden like the standard measure of all walks, with its uprights like centimeters; and, after our step was thus gaged, she left me, fleeing for the day toward a street, toward a single street, the Rue Pape-Carpentier, where by chance she had found a dentist, and thereafter, with her mind made up, all her other tradesmen.

Every evening she returned with some part of her repaired, and a purchase: a hat of red duvetine when her dog-tooth was filed; a fan of green *friseline* when her big toe-nail was set right. So, on the day when the artists of the Rue Pape-Carpentier delivered her from her hidden imperfections, she saw herself in the mirror quite made over, velvety and shining. At dinner I was subjected to her observations, which remained almost exactly the same as in Bellac, for in Paris she had preserved the hearing of a provincial: the funeral bell had tolled at Saint-Germain; lightening had struck in the Rue Danton; the weather-vanes on the town-hall of the seventh district were stuck, it was necessary to go as far as the Pantheon to learn the direction of the wind. Sometimes quarter-masters on leave approached her in order to sell trinkets. She bought a Japanese doll to carry to Japan; intending doubtless to release it there as one would a bird. And from her dentist she got a thousand important instructions for our travels: the Siamese have red teeth; the Annamites who have black lacquered teeth are not Annamites at all, but Tonquinese. These facts were pretexts for her to speak to me of her second fiancé, who, on the morning of his departure for Indo-China, had said to her—last words, supreme farewell; he adored her, the poor man: "You were stupid and bad tempered, and then you grew ugly!"

I, who did not know Paris, looked with dignity

and no enthusiasm at this city—so suitable for a point of departure—which is for every one the point of arrival, the spot where people from all the world finally let go their valises, like tumblers in a circus, feeling themselves free and exuberant for the first time in their lives. I was kept away from famous monuments by the same modesty which turns young people from great men. I turned away from the Arc de Triomphe, which Americans put on their souls like a binocular in order to see France; and I loved my short-sightedness. The Arc de Carrousel, standing abandoned like a palaquin in the desert, I left to the Sweedish and Danish; they could search around it for the bones of the animals which had brought it, and had then died there. Confronted by all these stones which were the personification of glory—the Vendôme column, the Bastille, the expiatory chapel,—I suffered from the same irritation, the same sense of deception, that one experiences in a petrified forest: these glories were rigid here, but their shadow still undulated and palpitated in Bellac. At the Louvre, in those pictures to which young boarding-school girls come for the sake of contemplating their supreme image in Cleopatra or in Judith, it was my own image in traveling dress that I contemplated most often;

and Scandinavian æsthetes could not understand
why I adjusted my waist, or why I tightened my
belt in the presence of a nude Antiope. I looked
at those Venitian canals, Lombard glances which
always come straight toward you, emptying in your
heart without a pause, gutters from a country
heavily laden with clouds; and I looked at those
executioners who manage to cut a ray of sunlight
just before the head of a saint. But I regarded
them with no insistence, like postal cards of a
country that I would one day see myself. Or, all
these pictures hung one beside the other moved me
to happiness in general, as posters in a station move
one to travel. Or they decorated my week of departure for me. Suddenly at the very idea of
Rubens I was gay; like the passenger who sees from
the Harve boat, doubling the mole, a fat Normand
woman running along the quai. Before Rembrandt
I felt a sudden thankfulness at the thought of a
great soul devoted to men; like one who, as he lifts
anchor for the Indes, sees a bearded petty official
save a child from the sea. Or I was as happy as
though it were Delacroix who had taken my ticket,
Manet who had registered my trunks; and the idea
of Watteau or of Chardin came to rest on my valise
or my dressing case . . . But that was all . . .

3

My heart which had been tossed skyward by the Champs-Elysées, held at the four corners like a blanket (the Checks at least assert it), was calm within me. On the battlements of Cluny, on the faces of the Rodin statues, it did not bite,—a wheel without teeth. Ascending the Seine, I returned slowly by the Boulevard Raspail, and far from wishing to know the crowds at the railway stations— those Egyptians, Australians and Japanese who arrived so painfully at this landing stage from which we were departing—it seemed to me that I was going into some marvellous double of their insipid countries, unknown above all to themselves.

In the afternoon I went to Chatou, to Joinville. I took trams which left the Seine, squeaking more than hydroplanes, only to win the Marne or the Oise, and which brought me back again each evening to the Alma, to the Concorde, to the heart of Paris and to sea level. Until we reached the gates of Clichy, Ivry and Vincennes, I remained in my mistrustful corner. But when the wall of Paris lay behind us, no longer anything more than a wretched tire burst in twenty places, which would have still required much blowing to make it round and hard; once the conductor had called out the names of those great men which, to the exclusion

of all other names, stop the trams suddenly
in the suburbs—Lakanal, Carnot, Zola; once we
had passed the railing of the dog's cemetery,
through which one saw old ladies clad in imitation
fur with feather boas of palm leaves, and footgear
of banana leather, who were death on all growing
things, weeding astonishingly dissimilar tombs on
which parrots, elephants and greyhounds alternated;
once we had cleared all those incredibly open spaces,
where all crimes are, however, committed, where
one feels, in this freight station for emptiness and
impalpability, the mingling of wireless telegraph
waves, where the meridians have their switches, and
where, heaped up in invisible packages, are all the
incorporal bundles addressed to Paris; once passed by
automobiles driven by fat parvenus, who hold the
wheel with the two little fingers lifted, like cocottes
when they drink; past the big advertising bill-boards,
shining or going to decay in the neighboring fields
according to whether their advertisers are making
money or going bankrupt; past a stream in a hollow, which, prouder than the Mississippi, is carrying on a single eddy a clump of briars toward a
tavern; at the limit of the zone reached by local
telegrams,—a place of sad villages, drenched in
perfume, treeless and without bushes, where soap

is manufactured, where the only birds are escaped
canaries; once past the file of little villas which are
so new that when one cries aloud the names inscribed
on their marble plaques—Mado, Nadine, or Colette
—one calls to the window the woman who inhabits
them, or one sees, in front of the cottage named
Hydrangeas, a stalk of hydrangea, the sponsor, set
in a stone or onyx pot in the center of the garden
and cherished like a fountain; then, when the road
turns straight east, and the elms and the advertisements of Benedictine, bent over by the north wind,
suddenly lean toward you; when the road turns back
toward the north and all the sardine tins gleam in
the soil, directly lighted by the sun; when a band
of small girls (the same who tasted their tears as
soon as they heard they were salt) fling themselves
behind the train in order to feel the rails because
they have been told they get burning hot; when the
river, which the tow-boat cuts exactly in the center
so that the wash will treat both banks alike, cuts
the plain at random, treating my heart at random;
when the Zouaves of Rosny come toward the
river from afar off, the best swimmers marching
the fastest; when a stream more worthy than
the Orinoco carries toward the river, on waters
irised by benzine, lemon peels and a red and green

canoe named *Youpinskoff;* and when, as the road
suddenly passes between cliffs, one sees overhanging
the acacias, at the top of the bank, the last spikes
of a great wheat field, the nearest wheat spikes to
the city; then, like a young girl who receives and
understands everything that borders passion and
friendship without wishing to understand either
passion or friendship itself, I understood all those
things, and closing my eyes I felt within them my
salt tears, without understanding Paris!

Sometimes I saw another young girl, an advertise-
ment for nature. I would smile at her and signal
to her. She would answer me from a distance by
shaking her head, by waving her arms, by one of
those gestures to which a deaf-mute abandons himself because his language is so empty. Sometimes
I saw them motionless, framed by a window or a
door, like one of those marks which formerly indicated, unknown to the owner, that everything within
should be plundered or respected; or they were bent
over in pairs, feeding a bullfinch. Others were
expelling their breath without ever inhaling deeply,
like inexperienced smokers, scarcely remembering
to breathe, condemned to death at the first moment
of forgetfulness. There was one who resembled
me, whose every look and movement could be ex-

plained only by an intractable frankness; another who resembled me quite as much, whose movements could be explained only by a limitless hypocrisy; and others who smiled at me sympathetically, so that I felt at once possessed and deprived of the password. But one day I saw that I was followed.

A young man was following me. If he wished to know the secret of young girls he was in luck. Every day he waited for me, near the hotel, in front of an anatomical shop which had polished lungs, wax livers, and half-severed heads in the window, but which exhaled an odor of fresh bread as there was a bakery in the basement. The baker was visible below the skeletons, white from head to foot, colorless and fat, a well-fed phantom. As soon as I had passed, the young man escorted me at a distance, thereafter indifferent to human beings, their limbs, their eye-balls, and the muscles of their knee-pan. But he caressed cats and dogs, and there was always a big Newfoundland at the door of a café, so affectionate that he fell completely over on the side which was caressed. Before long the young man dared to take my tramways to their terminal points; inspecting the bumpers which stopped them at Bonneuil or at Creteil; returning with me on the opposite bench, over a rail which was not mine, as near to

me and as far from me as one life is to a parallel
life. He was subject to the same police regulations
for omnibuses, to the same whims of the conductor
as I was, and sometimes, out of a hundred thousand
numbered tickets, he had the number directly following my own; but I no more thought that he
could speak to me than that our rails could intersect.
Sometimes I outstared him, and coldly turned my
glance from him to the extra-urban tariffs. Sometimes he affectedly turned his eyes to a spot on the
countryside: then I was sure, if I followed his
example, to see some pool or some bizarre villa.
Sometimes he turned his whole body, warning
me of something still more important: a château,
or a ruin. Sometimes he raised his eyeglass; he
insisted; and I felt—as I used to feel sitting beside
my grandmother's coachman—that he was turning
my head with his hand toward bell towers and
churches. Then I would resist, and sacrifice as
the price of my liberty the sight of a donjon
or a cathedral. Then—one must amuse oneself—I
played with him our boarding school game which
consists of treating the most indifferent creatures
with the words and gradations of passion itself.
I was satisfied to see him snapped at by a conductor,
for having nibbled his ticket after folding it in

quarters and rolling it; I was charmed to see his
reflection in the window behave toward my reflection more properly than he behaved toward me,—
despite the stories we had been told at Bellac.
I was heartbroken and overcome to see that he
had neither beard nor moustache; I was beside myself when the conductor forced him to pay a second
fare. At bottom all this meant nothing to me, and
once back in Paris I left him between his bread and
his cadavers without giving him another thought.
I was a trifle vexed, however, at being followed not
for my own sake, but, like a pointer, for the sake
of some game or other, of which I felt his shooting-
bag was full when the customs officials questioned
him at port. At last a day came when he did not
appear, nor the day after; but, all in all, I was
satisfied to be alone at last; I was charmed to feel
the reins loose on my neck; I was overcome with
delight when I sat down at the edge of the Marly
horse-pond without finding in the water opposite me
the reflection of a stranger; I was beside myself at
having grazed the friendship of a man and then
lost sight of him forever. At bottom I missed him
a little, and—like great tennis players or ball players
when they no longer have a gallery—I played badly
with Paris when I was deprived of my spectator: I

carding her lofty and mocking manner. She resembled him slightly. Before me was a very simple spectacle, a family meeting of fiancés or cousins; or something frightfully complicated, an adultery or an incest. Through the garden railings I looked at this monster without any of the sentiments which I had stored up against a day of meeting being of the slightest use to me,—as was the case with the first lion that I saw. I watched them sideways, a little shamefaced despite everything; not unlike those provincials who entrust themselves to a Parisian banker, suddenly expending on this unknown pair all the devotion which had been scrimped sou by sou in Bellac at the expense of Limousin hearts. And before long, if there had been a fourth spectator with an eye more powerful than mine, he would have credited the young man with two doubles instead of one. I went toward him, and he watched my approach, smiling and without surprise, like one who is accustomed to have the universe furnish him with friends and taxis. Satisfied with me, or with himself, he received me in this public garden as a child who comes toward another group to play at liberty, hypocrisy and frankness. I, at once satisfied and displeased that my pretty profile should be turned toward the girl instead of toward him, was stupid enough to ask the way to the Boulevard Gambetta.

"How lucky," he said, "we are going there. You have stumbled on two persons who are leaving for the Boulevard Gambetta. Come along. Our carriage is over there."

I followed. His friend Anne followed us; but I saw that when she got into the carriage she was no longer wearing her rings or her ear-rings. There was a slight crackling in her dress, the chink of turquoises.

. . . .

When Anne and Simon learned of my approaching departure, they wanted to have me meet their travelled friends one evening. I saw arrive—at long and short intervals, and as though it were the finish of contestants in a race around the world —a very blond, plump young man, whose skin was crackled by China but still pink, who was the Duke of Sarignon; an old Jewish actress from the *Français*, who spoke with an English accent, named Ceorelle; an aged explorer, remarkable anywhere by reason of his double dog-teeth who was the only one who appeared to have drawn a native profit from his travels, for he had pearls in his ears, a coral chain, buttons made of bat's

teeth, and photographs of Laplanders in his pocket;
and the Princess Marie Bellard, who was always so curious and so astonished at what the others
had to say that one wondered what road she
had been able to follow around the world by which
she escaped at once Siberia, the Indies, Brazil, and
the United States. But she recovered herself a little
at the isthmuses—Suez, Singapore, and Panama—
knowing the name of each company president who
had received her at the entrance of each canal. Last
of all came a tall thin personage on a very round
friend,—Toulet on Curnonsky.

The explorer flung himself upon the oysters.
Nothing more unfortunate, he declared, than the
oyster famine in the centre of Thibet! It was
apparent that he would invent an anecdote to go
with every course. But Toulet, who had taken a
dislike to him at his first word, halted him at the
soup, just before the description of the Kirghizes's
wedding soup (which is always served boiling outside the tent, and, which, thanks to the temperature,
ends as a sherbert). Toulet heaped insults upon
him. He proved to him, having procured a dictionary from the *maître d'hôtel,* that despite his
statements Canada is larger than the United States;
and then, requisitioning the hemispheres from a

chamber-maid, showed that the explorer's famous trip by way of Siberia, Alaska and the Hudson did not approach in kilometres one-quarter of the trip by way of the Equator. When the explorer defended himself, Toulet reminded him tartly that he had dedicated his travel book to Soleillet, and then proceded to make delicate allusions to another Soleillet, who had just killed a little girl, pretending to confuse the two. When his opponent still persisted, Toulet showed him that he was perfectly aware that the poor man had been suddenly moved to travel because of the misconduct of his wife; and when the explorer mentioned the names of Perm, Irkutsk, or Vancouver, Toulet regarded him with an expression at once furious and contemptuous, as though this white-bearded man were blushlessly avowing the various stages of his matrimonial misfortunes. At the word sledge Toulet was more indignant than any prelate ever was at mention of the vilest toilet article; at the word pemmican he blushed; and the more stubbornly the unfortunate man insisted on telling us of his overland journey from Asia to America, in a temperature of sixty below, the more Toulet's expression made us believe he was retailing an unworthy and discourteous story about his wife. Toulet was so successful that Curnonsky, by a natural transition, imitated for us the love song of the Labuan women which they sing when their lovers wish to depart for Borneo by tram and the husbands hold them back with flowers.

It was the 14th of July, and the whole company ascended to the roof to see the fire-works. Seated in steamer chairs on the sheet-iron terrace as on a homeward bound vessel, all these French people who had escaped from the Pacific watched the firing of a more beautiful signal than any captain ever sent flashing from his sinking ship . . . Toulet had the explorer's cigar extinguished, explaining that the light inconvenienced him and troubled the darkness between fire-works . . . The gas lamps around the Institute and the Louvre revealed the true architecture of these palaces, the true skeleton . . . Ceorelle's fiery necklace and her flaming rings likewise seemed to correspond to unfamiliar bone circlets, or to short round bones, different from ours. When she heard a cry in the crowd she trembled, pretending that a rocket stick would surely fall on someone's head and perhaps pierce it if it fell vertically; and after each detonation she counted as one does for thunder, feeling safe when she reached twenty. Marie Belliard, a drug addict, turned her little nose curiously toward the Duke de Sarignon.

who did not merit so much honor as he had merely washed his fountain pen in ether. The Duke spoke to us, from his knowledge of Chinese rites and French distances, in a varying voice and with different degrees of respect according to whether we were red, white or green (there were only these three colors, even for July 14th, as the fire-works were Italian). I listened to Toulet describe the sky and the fires by names of colors with which I was unfamiliar—advanturine, *itera, latil*—in a voice so caressing and insinuating that he seemed to be painting my eyes. There were some who spoke when the rocket rose, some who spoke when it had burst. Ceorelle, rigid with fear, struck the seconds as strongly as a country clock; and the explorer uttered a little cry, only one, at the exact moment of the explosion. Pursued by Toulet, he had found refuge only in this illuminated second.

Toulet was now beside me, with Curnonsky at his right, in the place that he had maintained throughout their trip around the world. Curnonsky, slightly bent, appeared to be searching with his near-sighted eyes for a signature in the right-hand corner of every thing and every spectacle, for the signature of the pyramids, of the baobabs . . . Toulet never yielded him the central position . . . With that cruel hand which had thrown a thousand dollars worth of lobsters to the octopuses in the aquarium at Malacca—in order to see the carapaces, which had been snapped to the bottom by the suckers, return empty at the speed of a bullet,—Toulet followed the flight of each rocket as it was sucked up by the night. I felt satisfied at being near him. When one talked with Toulet for ten minutes— clockmaker of souls that he was—one felt assured of running accurately for twenty-four hours: one committed no more pleonasms, no more solecisms, and no longer obeyed false syllogisms. And I was troubled a little only by his eyes inspecting my lighted face, repairer that he was, too, of sundials!

He asked what province I came from, and thereafter set himself to talk to me of Limousin as if it were not the land which I had left but my goal, and a distant Eden. Every word which I had to say about Bellac, Fursac and Chateauponsac, he took for some compliment that I had payed him; bowing at the word Eymontiers; blushing (with pleasure this time) at the word Crozant; or, as at a revelation, kissing my hand at the word Rochechouart; shaking it at the word Ambazac;—so that I did not dare to speak to him of my favorite villages. Amusing myself by a childish game—

4

which consisted in adding to all my replies, but
inaudibly, an avowal to the person who was talking
with me and who pleased me—I revealed to him
that among all our hills (good old Toulet) there is
neither sandstone nor lava, as Reclus asserts, but
little lakes; and he opened his lips with pleasure as
one does when he discovers that a bonbon, which
has been announced as nougat, is full of liquor. I
told him that the rocks of Blond (Toulet with the
beautiful hands) groan in autumn; and he thanked
me, as if he had learned from me not the word
Montagne-de-Blond, but the word *lament,* the word
autumn. I informed him that the shepherd girls
(adorable Toulet) strike their wooden shoes against
each other in order to drive off wolves; and he had
the appearance of a freed man, as though he were
going to profit by this recipe as soon as he reached
his parish near Saint-Augustin. Then—just as a
Paris modiste will take a Limoges hat from you,
retrim it, and replace it on your head—Toulet returned to me an elegant country in which I scarcely
knew myself.

He managed to lodge a great man in each one
of my commonplace towns. This province that I
had described to him so proudly (I was now confused), electrically lighted even in its tiny farms

and pigsties, was now lighted by him with genius.
In Limoges he lodged Renoir, compelling me to
disclose the fact that my grandparents were married at the time he was painting porcelain there;
that their coffee and table services had most certainly been decorated by Renoir. In Bellac itself
he placed La Fontaine, who was in love with a
young widow living there; very probably, he
assured me, an ancestor of mine. In Bessines he
located the Englishman Young and Yversen the
Danish woman, the friend of Chopin. The latter
was in love with a young citizen—blonde of course
—who was beyond all shadow of doubt my grandfather. So it was not long before I was, in his
eyes, the one descendant of France's greatest poet
and the most beautiful romanticist of Europe. And
he treated me as such. He kept his eyes closed, for
the artificial fire was tiring to them now. I saw
suns turning from left to right, moons turning from
right to left, and Henry IV on horseback, like a flat-
iron that was being pressed over the smooth Seine.
Toulet spoke to me from a knowledge as distant
as that from which old men speak to children: after
a silence, praising Bertrand de Born, the Limousin
troubador, commending him after all for having
employed only one metaphor in all his work; after

another silence, saying everything possible, affec-
tionately, sensibly and equitably, about kaolin and
pâte mi-tendre; after another silence, uttering the
eternal truth about salmon and chestnut trees. And
I was vaguely happy and blissful, rocked gently in
my country as in a cradle.

Fireships were now going down the Seine. Paris
was attacked by a false conflagration, covered by a
real smoke, and the shadows of its monuments were
consumed one by one. Little Sarignon had taken
me by the arm, and was telling me—I don't know
why—all those things by which one consoles an
abdicating king (excepting the kings of France):
that Paris alone is beautiful,—Paris and Versailles;
—Paris, Versailles and Marly; he was unable to
check himself,—Paris, Versailles, Marly, and Saint-
Cloud. Then everything was black, as in those fine
theatres where the scenery is changed without
a lowering of the curtain; and, with the noise of
great waters, under pressure of the accumulated
night, the jets flashed from the last fire-works; fountains rising from the most petrified spots in Paris,
from the plaster of Montmartre, from the pavement
of the Pont-Neuf, from the marble of Père-Lachaise.
All these expensive flashes, all these artificial flashes
stirred in me imperceptibly, but stirred at least, all

that was awakened in me by a flash of real lightening at Bellac: those desires, that minimum of desires (dear Sarignon) for a twentieth death, a third sex, a thousandth life.

With the old explorer behind us, stealthily twisting Ceorelle's hair as goblins do the mane of a filly; with Simon and Anne who were smiling at me, red, green and blue by turns, as though indicating different states of friendship; between Marie Bellard —who was reputed a bit of a liar, who murmured to me: "I detest you," and who smelled like "An olden day," a promising perfume on her—and the little duke, who now, with real tears in his eyes, was giving me all the practical counsel that is offered kings when they accede to power—that beauty alone is beautiful, truth alone true; with Curnonsky in the corner, the right-hand corner, searching with his eyeglasses for the signature of this night; with all the houses at the water's edge, carrying all their inhabitants in the angle of their highest terrace, as though they were going to plunge them into the river and be rid of them forever; with women crying to us from the street, as they cry from the windows to those on the ground during real fires; then, with Toulet beside me like Asmodeus, I awaited some unknown subtle and infernal science of Paris. And indeed he raised his arm, and he . . . Alas! night returned; there was no longer anything to be heard but the baying of a dog, as in the country; and all the astronomers were already crowding about their telescopes to turn them on a sky that had been so thoroughly shaken.

Everyone accompanied me, for I left for Saint-Nazaire the next morning. And when I opened my window I heard Toulet who, with all his strength, was striking his box-wood cane against the rhinocerous-hide cane of the explorer to bid me a last farewell and to scare away wolves.

CHAPTER III

I T was Sunday. Exchanging gods, the sailors
went to hear mass in the churches, and the citizens
went to the ships. I was embarking. Between my
ship and the quai lay two metres of incompressible
ocean, and there were two metres of light between the
edge of the sea and the horizon. Travellers returning
from Damascus and leaving for Oceania watched
with emotion, as symbols of a wandering life, the sea-
gulls which had never left Saint-Nazaire. The sunlight was sparkling. Pennants and the flags, doubled
for the holy day, beat the air; and one felt that the
epithet for each element and each creature was
doubled: the ship was white, white; the.sea was
blue, blue. Alone, abandoned on the dock in the
midst of her luggage, a pretty little woman—instead
of being brown, brown—was brown, rose. I offered
her my porter, who was rid of my big trunk, and
who at the sight of her little bundles was already
moving his arms toward them like a compass needle:

"My sister Sofia is looking for one," she replied.

Fed with fine leather trunks, the ship was already trembling and uttering little whistles. I suggested searching for Sofia.

"My husband Naki is looking for her," she replied.

I waited for awhile. Then I suggested searching for Naki.

"Riko, my brother-in-law, is looking for him. We have a ticket from the sub-prefect calling for the deck cabin that my cousin Papo once had . . ."

It was at the word *Papo* that I ceased to resist, that I was snatched up, that this little Greek woman caught me in the endless wheels of her relatives: I asked if Papo had gone far away.

"Papo was going to Rancagua in Chile to rejoin my aunt Marie. She is now living at Lima."

"Does she like it there?"

In this manner did my new friend—in a second's time, and with one word—compel you, under penalty of being impolite, to ask for news regarding the widow of a Liminien judge, and a druggist of Monastir. Thereupon I had to listen to Aunt Marie's latest letter, which told of her trip to the Andes and waxed ecstatic at the sight of a flock of llamas rising up from the snow under which they had been sleeping, with their high heads which

lightening strikes sooner than a man's. Uncle Lili
had photographed the rock from which the three
Inca brothers had departed, whose father . . .

For everything, past or present, in Nenetza's mind
was linked up with family affairs; and among
the gulls which were flying around us she distinguished father, mother, and children. Among
the boats which came and went she appeared to
imagine connections as natural as those of conception
and child-birth. Then the handsome Naki arrived—
twice as tall and broad as his wife, throwing her
into shadow like a wall—with a good soul whose
pennants, one felt, were doubled this fine Sunday.
He was calm, calm; he was strong. But his wife
Nenetza, his mate, his companion, remained sweet,
bitter . . . Having insulted Riko and kissed
him fifteen times on the mouth, she jumped into
our fat cousin of a ship, whose name she always
pronounced in entirety,—*Amélie-Cécile-Rochambeau*
—for she employed the friendly or loving diminu-
tive only in the case of masculine names. Already
a large cloud was threading its way out to sea, as
though it were going to judge the finish in a little
foot-race between friends.

An hour later I came upon Nenetza kneeling by
the netting, watching the farewells. She remained

insensible to separations which appeared rending, and was moved and stricken at the sight of people who simply clasped hands; for she distinguished unerringly between filial tears, fraternal tears, and tears that were merely avuncular. And she continually questioned the steward and me with phrases which were simple enough but which required some poetic answer, like those of sister Anne.

"Who are those hundreds of travellers, without baggage, who are boarding the other ship?"

"They are convicts leaving for Guinea."

It was, indeed, a file of convicts, two by two. A scrap of a torn letter fluttered to earth, and all of them elbowed one another a little and slowed down their step trying to read it.

"Who is that lady who is so beautiful and bold?"

"She is the *senora* Subercaseaux, from Bahia, who is travelling with her monkeys. She is the only a woman who has bred chimpanzees in a cage. For the birth of the last one a moving picture camera was brought in . . ."

Now we were leaving. As if I had filled my lungs too strongly with this new air and had then exhaled it, I felt this new soil move. The boat returned the captain's wife—a last anchor—to land, and turned in little curvets like a horse that is being saddled. Instead of ringing for luncheon, according to custom, the steward rang for mass as it was Sunday. Some famished persons were deceived by this and arrived with surprise, mouths watering, in the presence of God. It was a real mass, conducted in the dining saloon by a Lazarist returning to Peru, who had with him, as a special mark of favor to his order, the sacred vases. Naki refused to attend. Nenetza taunted him, asserting that the soul is immortal; then, disconsolate at learning that she had not seen the dolmen on the square of Saint-Nazaire, she scorned the last grass, the last church, the crowd in Sunday dress, and sought only to catch a glimpse of the saddest and most worn-out stone in Europe. Her neighbors, seeing her so sad and so disturbed, pitied her, not guessing that she was merely parting from an unknown dolmen. But already the last of the sparrows who had come to pilfer from the deck were flying away . . .

"Love!" said Nenetza.

Two belated drunken cooks ran along the mole making gestures and grimaces at the ship. Some children imitated them and stumbled. From our position all the people who remained ashore seemed mad, they appeared to be walking on error. We ourselves were already resting on the only truth. To starboard, in the middle of the sea, arose a great solitary cloud, sister of the dolmen.

"Love!" said Nenetza.

This was the word by which she replied to all the attentions of nature, to the flying fish, to the floating birds. I asked her why she employed this word: she told me that it was not a tic, that she really thought of something like Love . . . At least it was thanks to this little Greek that I left for another world as for a coasting voyage, innocently; trying to see all of France, like an island, as I left it behind . . .

We were leaving. All the passengers who, not believing in a too vengeful God, had skipped mass, were able to see Europe disappear. We skirted it from afar off, escorted on our right by the convict ship, sinister because it seemed empty; then suddenly swarming with heads,—coming up for exercise no doubt—so that one felt oneself convoyed to starboard by a ship which carried crimes themselves. The first beauty spots, made by cinders, were already gleaming on the faces of the two sweatered women passengers who were walking ceaselessly arm in arm around the ship. From an armchair one could tell whether it was cold or blowing by merely observing the cheeks and hair of this pair. The handsome Naki engaged steamer chairs for us on the deck, and everyone arrived with coverings or fur robes of the color he would have chosen for himself had he been an animal,—violet, with brown stripes, or gray with red spots,—contending for places where a clear sight of the ocean was not spoiled by a thread of iron or a sliver of cordage. Poor innocents! transported with delight at finding themselves free in a superb space, which the stewards knew, from ten years' experience, to be uninhabitable; uniting, no one knows why, the inconveniences, heat, cold, and bad odors, of all the continents.

Mademoiselle was learning nautical terms from a book—which I made her recite to me every evening —and was studying a chart of the heavens, in case the ship should be wrecked and the command of it should descend to her after the death of all those better qualified. The captain walked about, with his head screwed over on one side like an instrument for observing stars, and studied the various groups with an eye which seemed threatening but which was only hunting for poker players. All those little native threads by which Nenetza, without suspecting it, had attached me to everything French,—to bell-towers, to tramways,—began to pull a little. Already farther away from this land which we touched with our glances than from American soil, we felt all our European trees—the most luxuriant of which were still visible—range themselves in our memory in the order of their height: oak, elm, poplar, and birch; and all those sentiments which grow on the earth in thickets: love, friendship, pride; and of all French animals it was the largest which accompanied us farthest in thought: bulls, horses, oxen,—with heads raised for us above this water that they did not drink. Play had begun among the passengers, on the deck as on a chessboard; each one advancing according to the convention imposed by the sea; with little steps like a mere pawn, or at a bound like the Queen, or sideways like a knight. Nenetza and I were magnetic pawns who rushed toward each other; and we collided painfully.

The wind blew from the west for two days, opposing the ship as it made the turn around Europe. Sometimes the vessel sank down suddenly and then rose again, whereupon Mademoiselle gave the helmsman the glance with which one punishes a chauffer who has not foreseen a "thank-you-marm." After the first day we rejoined the large cloud which had left two hours before us, and every evening it gathered our sun up in its wadding. Beside Mademoiselle's chair, an empty chair—abandoned by a sick passenger—received all the passengers who liked to change places and unknown persons who sprang up suddenly at night. Sometimes it was Sophie Mayer from Munich, who was going to rejoin her fiancé, an inventor at Bogota; clad always in blue dresses, foulards and bright blue stockings, often invisible against the netting. She was studying the grammars of the countries which the ship skirted: French, until a fold in the sea made her take up her Spanish grammar,—assured that she would not address her saviours in solecisms were she shipwrecked. Sometimes she was shaken by a shiver which must have corresponded to some inventive tremor in her fiancé. Presently it was M. Chotard of Valpariso, whose tie was secured by a black pearl which had remained in his hand from a necklace of Tahiriri, the daughter of Pomparé, whom he had caught as she was falling from a veranda, on that day—fifty-nine years ago—when he had brought her mother a pair of yellow boots which the Empress Eugénie had sent as a present. Then it was *senora* Subercaseaux with her monkey stories, and Kikina, her chimpanzee, a sister of Lirila who had found the black spectacles of Father Antonio in the chapel park, and, after putting them on, had broken a new statue from Lourdes, dying mad that same evening when night fell—still darker than the spectacles—for the edification of the hacienda slaves. Then it was a tall, red-haired Norwegian, who in his gasoline launch had overtaken a wing of the hospital on the pilings at Colon which had been about to drift away, and who Naki insisted was in love with his wife.

"Hasn't he a right to be?" asked Nenetza.

"And why did you choose me from among all the tennis players of Delos?"

My soul grew fat on salt and rest. All my feelings for France became enfeebled; and on the contrary there stirred in me—still slight as yet—sudden and definite desires: I wanted to save a young Greek woman from shipwreck, to make a Norwegian weep, to oblige a girl from Munich to put on a red waist. . . . At times all the passengers precipitated themselves to one side of the ship because a little black boat, like a rat seen through a telescope, was lying between us and the setting sun. Sometimes a breath of eucalyptus reached us—we had anticipated it from afar by observing the noses of the two women in sweaters,—and Sophie Mayer searched for her Portugeese grammar. To starboard, instead of the convicts, instead of men who had killed their daughters, plundered cathedrals, there were now only little fishing boats innocent of any police record, and British colliers who held bishops in respect. The captain came and went, distributing among the distinguished passengers phrases which were very nearly incomprehensible, for he had the habit of forgetting in his speech those adverbs and prepositions which we sometimes forget in writing: "in regard to," "with," "since."

"They are quarreling a hat," he would say. "I came a dog . . . I waited for him a statue. . . ."

He put in at San Ioao under the pretext of taking on ice, but actually to pick up, and keep on board, Major Almira Peraira d'Heica, the famous poker player. This made it possible for four of us to go as far as Porto by automobile with the red-haired Norwegian and an English general who always replied "very practical." I remember towers of porcelain; a palm grove in which a young French woman was caressing a young palm; the Douro, green, green (very practical); the roofs, Chinese red, red; and the two suspension bridges with reflections going toward the river when an ox turned his head because of his leather diadem. It was the eve of the harvest; the youngest port was nearly a year old. It was the week when Porto's most foolish inhabitant, so far from new wine, is the wisest. At sight of us one of them cried, "Long live the democrats!" The guide explained to us that some one in Lisbon had cried, at the same time— so strong is the instinct of contradiction between the two cities—"Long live the liberals!" On the hills lay lines of little mills which ground the wheat grain by grain.

"Love!" said Nenetza.

"Very practical," said the general.

And we returned to the *Amélie* along avenues where the dust moved in special eddies instead of following the automobiles, where signs in front of each palace gave warning that the park was protected against marauders by means of explosive traps. . . .

It was a day of fog and disagreeable faces. The Gulf Stream now reached the hearts of only a few passengers. The sea appeared calm, but it threw the ship down as though it were falling over a cliff. Then a dry wind covered us with dust, as though we had been in a square of Tarascon. Sophie Mayer raved because she had no Arabian grammar. A shower fell, releasing from the ship—which had formerly been English, then Japanese, then German —all the odors which had accumulated in her, and the passengers fought them with a thousand various perfumes. At last, toward evening, the sky opened, and we saw above the masts some real stars, isolated and new, like those one sees at the movies when the roof of the hall is opened. The next day we sighted Madeira, where the captain stopped under the pretext of refilling with water, but actually to put ashore (regretfully, for it was the 21st, and he always held aces on the 22nd) Major Almira Peraira, swollen with money, amid hissing boilers. This gave us an opportunity of being drawn to the top of the island in a basket over a track of round pebbles. We had already left Europe behind. On the square at the left of the wharf the trees were the color of willows, the turf was blue, the streams red. Beggars beseiged the churches, the old ones counting on those going in, the ignorant children on those going out. The men passengers bought tobacco, the woman bought stamps; and we received as change pieces of bronze so heavy that they stretched out our clothes. The wind lifted the purple curtains of a gilded ox-cart, and the Norwegian was seen kissing Sophie Mayer. The naked urchins were of good family; those who were dressed had come in contact with the English: they were beggars.

On the trees beside each cluster of grapes was

a cluster of wistaria, and before gathering the fruit one had to touch the flower and stir its perfume. From the arsenal a cannon ball, dislodged by a clumsy sentry, came down the steep street all alone, slowing up at the stairway landings, pursued by the trumpet. Then the siren of the *Amélie* whistled, and the last European reflection smiled at me. On the face of a little girl who was kneeling on the quai I caressed the last European reflection; and Naki's strong arms tore me away from my land.

During two days Africa pushed out some islands on the sea, like a gambler's stake: the Canaries, the Cape Verde Islands. We disdained them. After this came the Southern Ocean, and each day was less than twenty-three hours long. The sun commenced at our outstretched feet; then like a dye it pushed the shadow little by little up our bodies, and at evening it left us baked and golden. Certain little facts, useful in adding pleasure to the passage, valueless after the voyage, were now definitely established: the Norwegian wished to live for me alone; I would always live with Nenetza; the general would raise a pair of kangaroos at Sydney for Juliette Lartigue. Thereafter easy in our minds, we went to mass every morning. It was conducted in the library by the head of the Grand Seminaire at Truxillo; the

ciborium was placed on top of two dictionaries—
torn from Sophie Mayer for each occasion—and the
fans of all the Liminien and Venezuelan women
rustled, except for an instant during the elevation of
the host.

At evening, when darkness had seized us, we
would borrow a violin from a second-class emigrant,
and Naki, accompanying himself, would sing in
Greek: "A sweet love, a beautiful isle," or, "It is
the very image of his father." Some Italians on the
prow played the mandolin with two emigrants from
Barcellonette who played the accordion. Then
Nenetza would beg us to go between decks to see
the three marmots; or the general, deeply moved,
would talk to me of France: he had always wanted
to see the little hill in the face of which the Loire
abandons going to the Channel and turns to the left.
From the deserted chair someone would get up whom
we had not seen stretch himself out there, whom we
knew only by a nickname: the rat man, the canteen
woman, or a Peruvian philosopher with a white
beard who discussed labor questions with Mayer.
This man when he wished to think in Peru took the
funiculaire and climbed to a height of five
thousand metres. The North star appeared, and the
Norwegian, following a straight line amid cordage

and under chains, took twenty quick steps toward it,—a reflex action of Scandinavians. The owl which came up from the hold every evening to fly around the ship—being greeted by the word "owl" in all the languages of the world—finally alighted: Mademoiselle's heart grew calm. By means of light signals our captain played poker with the captain of the prison ship. The whites of Naki's eyes absorbed the stars like blotting paper. The stars grew larger; the sky was pierced like a confessional, with a candle on the side of the Father, and we made our confessions, all of us complaining softly. I complained of Naki who pinched his wife's shoulder despite the promises he had made me. Chotard complained of the half-breeds of Iquique, where, on revolution days, he was compelled to have his maid escorted to market by a full-blooded Indian who fired on the windows. Naki complained of the Turks who had massacred his family every twenty years since the beginning of the era recognized as Modern by French history books. The general complained of the Balorabari, an Afghan tribe, who had stolen a house dog from him. Mademoiselle had her say about the bugs. Each moaned like a little beast about the beast his enemy.

The captain had just told us that we were at the

spot where the Gulf Stream makes its turn, and the curious general leaned over the side to try and see what little hill was responsible. Then the moon arose, and Nenetza, politely loathe to point at it, spoke to us about it, contending that the soul is immortal.

"I tell you it isn't," said Naki.

"Everyone knows it is. Isn't the soul immortal, general?"

The general had heard it affirmed at Oxford. At Cambridge they denied it; but a mortal soul would be so impractical!

Finally we would get up, almost lowering our heads because of the stars which were so close. Little wakes of fire could be seen coming at high speed from the convict ship where the plates and dishes were finished: they were sharks. After some slight desires—that of being a giant in order to scratch the sea at its irritated and burning spots, that of turning the helm, that of being Pizarro's niece; after a last look cast at the stars as at a coverlet prepared in advance, we would go below to sleep. Nenetza undressed me, and lifted up my foot in order to hoist me into my bunk as though I were a horsewoman. Then Mademoiselle slid in below me, clinging to the straps until morning—like Ulysses

under his ram—as though to escape from this night
of which she was always afraid. We heard a last
step; the Liminian philosopher was descending
from a height of ten metres in search of sleep. We
slept. Sometimes I was awakened during the night
by some unfamiliar thing, like remorse, or a fold in
the sheet: it was Nenetza's engagement ring which
I had put on in play and had forgotten to return.
Sometimes the port-hole window opened suddenly
like the door of a railway carriage when someone
enters.

A month passed thus. Before long we put into
some port every thirty hours: Venezuela, peopled
with huge stature all raised by Bianco, all of unknown Venezuelans who were, however, celebrated
because honored by Bianco; Martinique, in terraces,
with ruins, like a typewriter full of palms with two
or three broken letters; Colon, where the Norwegian
blushingly showed us the hospital annex on piles,
now secured by four chains; the canal, cut like a
tourron, with its tertiary embankments on the left
trying vainly to conspire with the secondary embankments on the right: then (everyone on board would
have described it thus) it balanced some empty
orange peels without letting them sink, it gently
withdrew two metres when it was pulled in the

direction of China, it licked the bare feet of the
light women of Panama who were crowned with
feather hats,—and even we would perhaps have
called it the Magnanimous, the Sure, the True
Friend,—it seemed to look at you from all its waves
with only a single eye, like the eyes of faces in
advertisements,—the Pacific!

.   .   .   .

Yes, it was just as you think. It was, indeed,
a midnight awakening: my hand which was reaching
downward toward the electric switch struck Mademoiselle's hand which was raised toward it. There
were light steps, so light that Mademoiselle believed
they were made by *senora* Subercaseaux's monkeys,
who had a passion for stealing tooth-brushes; and she
called them by their names—Kalhila, Chinita—the
tenderest names of Lima, capital of caresses . . . It
required her naïveté to hail death as Kalhila,
Chinita.

Yes, the port-hole window closed suddenly, taking
with it Mademoiselle's chemisette which was drying
after having been washed for tomorrow's celebration. She darted forward snatching at the linen
which had been ruined by a big patch of oil, gathering within herself as much indignation and contempt
for the Pacific as could be brought together in a

being who weighed forty-nine kilos and was one hundred and fifty-two centimetres tall. She held open the port-hole window like the eyelid of a giant who does not wish to see. He must have witnessed the loss of the chemisette, formerly celebrated for a day along the whole Rue Pape-Carpentier. He must have seen me, seated on my bed, as in the country when the dying neighbor is getting worse. A hissing rose from the ocean, like that of gas when it has been left on.

"The Equator!" said Mademoiselle.

Yes, the keys were falling suddenly from the locks, the paper cutter falling from Pascal which I was reading. The hand of the alarm-clock jumped, every object was freed from what made it humanly useful; the hand or the key to every phrase of Pascal fell on me who had understood. Pascal, Marcus Aurelius, and all the other gods of terra firma were impotent and useless.

"A phantom!" said Mademoiselle.

Yes, a sailor was entering our cabin, ordering us to dress, begging us particularly to put on our shoes, as though we had to make a long journey overland. . . .

"A mutiny!" said Mademoiselle.

She dressed in the presence of this placid Breton

as one would dress before a pirate, secretly fastening her gold chain, suppressing the noise of her snappers. Then the electric bulb flew into shivers. The sailor went out to hunt for matches. To each of us the other appeared like some shaken phantom, from whom some unsecured object—a piece of small change, a buckle—was continually falling. From me especially: the repairers of the Rue Pape-Carpentier had been conscientious. By little insidious remarks I tried to discover whether my companion realized we were on the reefs.

"They are going to shoot the captain," she replied.

It was a race through the empty passageways, littered with glass and broken plates. Without the sailor's advice our feet would have been covered with blood.. Near the pantry we were compelled to trample on grapes and rotten mangos, and to hurdle cakes of ice. The seasons—traitors to mankind— also had their little say in this disaster. At last the sky appeared, the whole sky, so pure, so laden with stars that Mademoiselle cried out (it was almost her last word in this tempest) :

"Ah! What fine weather it is!"

Then she uttered a cry: we had forgotten our life belts. She ordered me to stay where I was, in front of life-boat number ten, where we had arrived first every Sunday morning for drill. The head-lights of three automobiles on the bridge had been lighted: under the stars this gave the illusion of a breakdown in the country far from any town. Seated on heaps of cordage, my head in my hands, stopping up my ears, closing my eyes, I wished to avoid fate and I refused to surrender to my senses, to accept irremediable signs. I tried in vain to gather around me everything which I believed eternal; and called up that logic which made it so improbable that a young girl from Bellac should have to die in the middle of the Pacific, and that modesty which forbade me to believe that a famous catastrophe was necessary for the annihilation of so feeble a con-sciousness. Under the awnings pianos rolled back and forth making a great racket.

"A fire," some one said in my ear.

For Mademoiselle had hit upon this last device of making the water seem less redoubtable to me. I looked at her. For she had gone to seek more than a belt; she had found other eyes, shipwreck eyes; other lips; other hands, gaunt hands, which one felt were assassins for all that might menace me. She drew the belt from a piece of cloth in which she had wrapped it, looking around her, and one guessed that during her ten-minute absence she had learned what crimes are committed for a life-belt. She wished to put the belt on me herself, turning me around in her arms as though we were dancing, with her head always turned toward the right or left, just as one watches one's rival in the tango. At last she attached it by a knot, not by a buckle,—the greatest sign of distress and of affection that she could have given me, for she had taught me for ten years to regard knots as detestable things, both useless and wrong since buckles exist. She kissed me from a distance because of the belt, bending her head forward as toward a pregnant woman, not wishing to graze my belt.

"Yours," I said.

She blushed and retreated.

"I found only yours."

I seized her by the arm; she pulled herself away as though we were already in the sea and she was afraid of weighting me down. I tried to tear off the belt: she looked at me, holding in her hand a little package for her sister, which she no longer dared entrust to me since I was so mad. I ran after her; then she leaped over the netting and cried to me (terrible confession) before disappearing:

"It's a tempest!"

.   .   .   .

Yes, it is just as you think. Nenetza was picking me up, kissing me. She scented me, for she had broken her bottle of perfume over herself. The most fragrant stream from the land, from Paris, enveloped me. She handed me her pearl necklace and one of her rings. Naki held me up; she undid her belt and attached it to me forcibly, for mine had been stolen during my fainting spell. Her sacrifice, her *sang-froid* assured her once for all of triumphing over Naki, and she reveled in it; she was happy to be right at last in those interminable contests which were their life. Naki's every movement, his eyes, his lips, proved that he no longer debated anything that she had ever affirmed: that Merika Arnagos was less beautiful than Basilea Persinellas, that the soul is immortal, that Bordeaux is as good as Burgundy, that starboard is on the left and port on the right. Nenetza brightened with gratification; then as I was calmed and was crying, she kissed me.

"Farewell, dearest," she said. "I smell too good, eh? Farewell my little Naki. You see that bottles of Coty are not solid. Farewell, beloved Naki. You see that there are tempests sometimes . . . Oh! Look at that star!"

We had lifted our heads: we lowered our eyes too late—she had jumped.

Yes, for hours, mornings, evenings, Naki was swimming at the edge of my raft. I looked at him for whole minutes; my one aid, all that remained to me, the man who was determined to save me, with his Greek accent. During the afternoon the sun compelled me to turn my head, and Naki, in order to feed my glances, made the circuit of the raft. Great blows could be heard at the bottom of the sea. We had a vague hope, like miners who are being rescued. I signalled to Naki to climb up on the raft: he placed a knee on it—I shall always see him thus—and threw himself backward with the movement of those little Greeks that one chases from the step of a victoria.

Night fell; I slept. Day returned; I awakened. The raft was enriched by all the stray objects which had come within Naki's reach; a whole collection which proved how confident he was, to the very end, of my escape. There were bottles so that I might drink when I was once ashore; an umbrella to furnish me shade in Oceania; a sort of fur robe so that I would not be cold when winter came. I was delirious with a delirium which urged me toward love, toward gratitude, like a patient awakening after an operation. I racked my brains for everything which I knew might please Naki, and I shouted it to him.

His frightful scarf-pin, of which he was so proud, was a rock-pearl, held by a gold snake, which was in turn held by a hand, a hand resting on an emerald tortoise: I cried out to him how simple and superb I thought it. I remarked how English was his tie from Smyrna; bright red with lilies and green borders. He thanked me with a movement of his head which brought the ocean just below his mouth. He suddenly swam up to me, caressing my dry face with his wet hand. How beautiful his cuff-links were, of malachite, girdled with dragons! How simple were his eyes of adventurine on ivory, framed by blue eyebrows, tufted like palms! And I did not understand why he held out his purse to me, like a lady who makes her guest pay for her in a restaurant, or why—for he had no imagination—he suddenly pointed out something in the sky to me, although it was day, and made me turn my eyes away from him for a second .   .   .

CHAPTER IV

I T was night. I must have remained unconscious for an entire day, for as far as I could reach with my hands I found myself dry and warm. I thought of thrusting my arm through the planks of the raft: it was land!

"Suzanne!" I cried.

It was not merely that I seemed, by this sand, by these pebbles, to rediscover proof of myself. Many times before I had touched land without crying aloud my name! But it was the word which Nenetza uttered on all occasions; and all the tricks of speech of the friends who had died to save me—the "I promise you," of Mademoiselle, instead of "I assure you"; the "to be in danger" of Naki when he meant to say "lose at play"—were in my ears throughout this night, as though they had been their dying cries. . . . My hand had encountered a root in the sand: I fell asleep without letting go of it,—my last cable . . .

"Very practical," I said as I awakened, still despite myself.

So it was that I learned of the general's death . . .

There was no moon. I sought in vain to find a footing in this opaque sky. I did not dare to leave my raft: on my right the sea came and went like a jointing-plane; at my left the island remained silent. Why an island? I do not know what indicated it to the touch. The hours ran on. I recognized each watch of the night from a noise which was unfamiliar, but whose translation I guessed. Toward midnight a trumpet sound and three hululus: that must be the first song of the cock. A little later what must correspond to our two o'clock breeze with its perfumes of jasmine and wistaria: a breath of vanilla, of pears. Then still later, the noise of kisses which made all the other birds keep silent, which must correspond to trills at home, to the nightingale. I dared not think. Occasionally two or three words crossed my brain, the word Night, the word Sea, as if all who had pronounced these two words had saved me and then died . . . Then a dry, warm breath: the equivalent of dew in this archipelago . . . Then the same anguish . . . Then a blow on my head; and a bird with a large beak fled after having wounded me; the blood ran down my forehead . . . This corresponded to Made-

moiselle's morning call. So it was that the island
awoke . . . A feeble moon listlessly passed a
whitish glaze over the whole sky; and suddenly the
sun, behind me, with a single ray, with one cloudy
rag, made everything gleaming . . . I turned
around and saw my island . . .

It was emerging from the mist. A thousand
rainbows, upright or aslant, joined the streams to
the hills. Groves of palm-trees, cut with carmine
foliage, shone in the humid air, more immobile than
zinc . . . Suddenly I heard the noise of waterfalls,
sounding like water-faucets that have been turned
on . . . Every tree liberated a red or golden bird
that it had held throughout the night as hostage for
the dawn. And ten metres from me I saw already
collected—so that all misunderstandings between
Providence and myself concerning this matter might
be dissipated after the first moment—everything that
was needful to appease my hunger and my thirst,
lying almost within reach of my hand, like a breakfast placed beside a sleeper. Banana trees offering
a thousand bananas like a thousand handles, the
best of which one broke off with the kindliness of a
surgeon who breaks a rib, with the same delight,
too, at the crack; cocoanut trees, higher than oaks,
from which the nuts fell on moss or on stalagmites,

bursting open in the latter case; mango trees,—and the first mango that I picked was exactly ripe. For thousands of years the race between my destiny and that of this mango had been timed to the second. A bright sun busied itself behind ferns and palms like a cook. Or, with rays separated and crossed like the chop-sticks of an eating Chinaman, it importuned me, showing me little pineapples and enormous strawberries. Everywhere were trees which were unknown to me, but which I guessed to be food riddles. Patience would serve to give me the solution, to tell me which among them was the bread-tree, which the milk-tree, which, perhaps, the meat-tree. Trees without fruit and almost without foliage, but banded with red circles, which I surmised full of abundance; and I tapped their trunks with my hand or with a stick to see if they were full. Trees which offered their gifts more frankly in proportion to their degree of sterility; holes from which bees flew out; holes from which honey itself was running; and even birds eggs in their nests, within reach of that human being who had never yet passed by. Turtles stopping in the shade but close beside a patch of sunlight which was hatching their eggs, like a male bird near its female. Among the shrubs, which one guessed were

spices, were grasses, which one guessed were
vegetables; flowers which I was instinctively
led to sample, that tasted like young pig and
were nourishing. Great flowers full of rain water,
from whose faucets I could drink through a straw
. . . and my hands, after one morning on the
island, carried as many scents as the hands of a bar-
maid after her first morning of apprenticeship at
the bar.

So that all misunderstandings between the Providence of perfumes and myself might also be dissipated, the breeze sprayed me with all the island
odors. There were some among them which were
familiar, which I found as pure as in the vicinity
of their bottles: *Rose d'Orsay, Ambre Antigue,
Mouchoir de Monsieur.* But the strange ones pre-
dominated, and smelling them for the first time they
stirred in me—in default of real memories—the
memory of a savage. ' They clung to you; you
guessed that they were not sterile as in Europe, but
that they settled on you in accordance with an end
chosen by nature. Each perfume pushed me away
from its shrub as though I had to flee from it. I
walked along, unknowingly following the length
of the island, going instinctively to the promontory
which had formerly attached it to a continent; and

suddenly I stood hopeless above a broken **bank,—** thousands of years late . . .

But life rose up in me with the day . . . **A** bright sun was attacking every flower and waterfall with a courteous lance. The humming-bird carried the perfume of the last flower visited and a beak **of** its color . . . Golden creepers, like pipes, linked the tree clumps, and appeared to circulate among **the** subscribing trees all the conveniences of Oceania. All the comfort, all the luxury that nature can give itself from personal pride in little unvisited islands was there: a little hot spring in agate rock near a little cold spring in moss; a geyser of warm water, which rose hourly, beside a fall of iced water; fruits similar to soaps; scattered pumice-stones; leaf-brushes and pine-pins; the simulacrum in golden quartz of a great Louis XV mantle and of an organ in a less pure style; a cavern of rock-crystal in which a red bird was sometimes caught, making it shine like an electric bulb; and—supreme island comfort— as in the depths of the store-rooms of Poiré and de Groux, there were in the depths of each straight glade, paved with black coral and bordered with cocoanut trees on which rose colored crabs climbed up and down, heaps of blue and red feathers massed against a little central hill. . . . It was indeed an

island. Wandering along the beach, seeking a ford
by which to cross the Pacific, I had circled it when
evening came. . . . It was, perhaps, two miles in
width, three in length; aslant in the ocean, from what
the sun told me. The same evening I had leaped
across the seven streams, having been compelled to
seek the source of the swiftest and the broadest; I
had climbed the mountain, and had perceived—so
that all misunderstanding with Hope, too, might be
dissipated after the first day—a second island,
slightly larger than mine, two or three kilometres to
the south; and, so that the road should not appear in-
finite to my glance, a third island, half way between
the second and the horizon, shining with large green
lights like the *arrets facultatifs* of the Paris tramways. . . .

.   .   .   .

I blush to confess how I passed my first week,
when I compare my frivolous life to that of classic
shipwrecked adventurers. Aside from the blow of
the beak which awoke me each morning; and which
ceased the day that I surprised and struck the bird;
aside from this blow on the forehead, which was
for anyone of my age scarcely stronger than a firm
thought, I did not experience a single pain on the
island. The second day I busied myself with mak-

ing, in one of the three niches of the white coral cave, a bed from the feathers with which the island was littered. The third day I withdrew the feathers which were too stiff and gathered the down which the big sea birds lost at the slightest flight, being plucked by a glance as by a charge of shot. On the fourth day I sorted the feathers according to their colors in order to have three divans, yellow, ochre, and red. The fifth day I was compelled to empty the three niches like three bath-tubs in order to recover one of Nenetza's rings that I had lost in them. The sixth day I pulled out certain green feathers which were fading, and certain purple ones which pricked me. After these six days of creation I had just succeeded in making my bed . . .

Already, however, milk had gushed for me from the milk-tree; stroking the trunk with my hand—thousand year old heifer whose mane the wind sometimes blew against my cheek—I succeeded in filling my preserve jar. Already I knew that one could drink immediately from the wine-tree, but that it was necessary to age the juice of the cider-tree; already I knew the fruits which should be dried and those that should be eaten fresh. Then,—after I had swept my beach with a broom of real marabou; when I had completed my dress of strings

and paradise feathers; once I had examined everything,—examined the sun with my two magnifying
glasses from which I drew fire most easily, examined the stream full of fish whose frolics were
limited to a stretch of two hundred metres between
salt water and the rock of the spring, examined
the three echoes, the last of which repeated your
words twelve times (an echo for women only), examined the oysters, the clams, which were excellent
but whose shells were soft because they were new,
examined the grass which for me would take the
place of chervil, the grass which would be my onion
—then, feeling myself eternally devoid of occupation on this perfect island, I waited . . .

So much the worse if I describe to you too soon
the tortures of waiting. I passed my days at the very
edge of the sea, my feet touching the ocean because
of an indefinable superstition which condemned me
not to lose contact with it. I waited for evening,
for the morrow at the latest. Sometimes, hopeless,
I recoiled a metre, a step: I did not expect to be
rescued before six months, before a year had passed.
By calculations—the figures of which I verified all
day long, sometimes gaining a week over the preceding total—I arrived at the exact number of
months, of years—barring an unlikely chance—

that I would have to endure this island before a
ship would be sent out to search for us. Better than
a shipowner who constructs his own steamer, I now
knew what a ship costs in labor and in days . . .
How many more weeks would it be before they
would refit mine; before they would have repainted
its red band (forseeing that the sun shines in Europe); before they would assemble between decks
the sailors whom I saw at that moment in the depths
of a tavern at Saint-Brieuc, or in a railway car from
the Gannat station, on the diagonal running from
Brest to Toulon which carries crews from one sea
to the other with Auvergne for a lock! How much
longer would it be before those sheep would be
put on board; sheep that were still pasturing in
Nivernais near some farm-house whose hedges
would be clipped before their sale! Six months of
continuous sunlight in Europe would help me by
two or three days! Sometimes I thought I felt that
the ship was ready to leave, that it was leaving; a
great ship was launched, the water came up to my
ankles. But a suspicion crept into my mind, a de-
fect crept into the vessel, and I felt obliged to turn
it back to port. I suddenly saw the Salers beef,
which should have filled its tins, still alive and un-
disturbed in a sunken road of Salers; I saw the

third ring of the starboard anchor abandoned on a lock at Creusot,—the workman had grippe, he was threatened by pneumonia . . .   Of all those infinitesimal objects which were more necessary in eternity than its boilers and its bulkheads, the pickle-bottle for the captain's table was still at the bottling works, the assistant doctor's double watch-charm was in the bottom of a watch-maker's drawer in Angoulême. How I wished that the second doctor had not had an automobile breakdown on that square in Angoulême, that he had not gone for a stroll, and that I had not been abandoned forever!

Finally my ship departed properly loaded; but suddenly it appeared too new to me. It was necessary that three kitchen glasses should be broken before departure; that two yards should be cut down (ah! may a storm blow swiftly over Europe); that a sailor should have a finger amputated, a passenger the lobe of an ear. In my haste I had gathered together a shining crew, but it was lifeless, it was composed of phantoms; and I put them ashore, delivering them to the bites and accidents of elevators, to the pricks of life! Sometimes a whole season raised itself against me: the ice for the pantry was still in some stream; the wine for the crew was still grapes . . .   Or, in mid voyage, the bird which had

left North Cape and which should have been sighted
by the watch off Newfoundland, the seaweed from
Cuba which should have touched the ship's keel, the
Patagonian tortoise which should have danced in its
wake off the Azores, did not reach the ship's course
on schedule, and all the threads of my destiny broke
under this impotent shuttle. So powerless is a
woman of central France to do the work of God, and
so surely must she give him back his task! . . . How
many times my heart was suddenly wrenched because
I had just seen, climbing an elm in Savoy, the wildcat whose fur would surround the neck of my
savior helmsman; or because I had seen, motionless
on the border of Dalecaria (against a background
of snow I could see no more than a few patches of
its bark), the birch tree which would furnish paper
for the first *Petit Parisien* that I would read on
shipboard.

At evening, when I was falling asleep while ru-
minating all possible rescues, there came to me new
calculations which I could not resolve. A savage
was indeed approaching the island, but he was in a
canoe which could hold only one person. A little
submarine appeared; but every one of its three
men was indispensable to its management, and there
was no extra place. A balloon was landing, with a

nacelle which held eleven persons; but every one
of them was indispensable—not to the management
of the balloon, this time, but to the lives of the ten
other beings—parts of a gearing more essential
than that of the crankshafts. I refused to separate
the captain's wife from her friend the mechanician;
or the doctor—who would die on the day that he
no longer had his proper diet—from the cook. I
did not wish to be the cause of so many disasters;
I renounced a place among them; and at such moments only the sight of the *Lusitania* would have
filled me with an unmixed joy. I fell asleep, no
longer having hope in anything save the largest
boat in the world.

At times I waited without speaking, without eating, without hoping, stretched out before the sea
like a dog before a tomb. What emotion did I
feel? The remorse of a child who has allowed
himself to be run over or to be lost. As to that, I
had always been sufficiently absent-minded and un-
systematic. At the edge of the Rhône I had discovered Joanne of the Loire in my valise and had
visited the Popes' château in a mood for Chenonceaux. During my second school year I had been
mad about third year authors, and had arrived at
examination not with Racine, Fénelon and Baude-

laire, but with Dante, Shakespeare and du Bellay;
with false witnesses who abandoned me in cowardly
fashion at the first contraction of M. Joubin's eyebrows. Now, in these mornings on my island, I
had the impression not of being separated from
everything but of having mislaid everything. So I
reached the age of twenty, not with pear trees and
nightingales, but with mahogany trees and cockatoos. I was at the wrong meeting place; I would
have to consult a travel agency and take a good boat.
In consequence I winked my eyes as I looked at
each tree, each bird, in order to replace them by
something truer, or to rob them of that exotic form
which can be given them in Europe only by winking
one's eyes. I had mislaid bread, wine, and hors-
d'œuvres; I had mislaid men, children, women; I
had lost animals and vegetables. What confusion! . . . From the top of a rock I saw the trees
with their weighted limbs, the creepers with their
ends lost as in the reverse side of a tapestry; I had
turned my life wrong side out; I had turned the sea
over on its barren side . . . I waited . . . Already,
in this eternal time, everything was dissociated from
my past. Whereas during the first months I set
aside hours for prayer, for sleep, and for meals,
whereas I had felt obliged to eat breakfast, dinner

and supper every day; I now lived on bananas or mangoes hour by hour. In the middle of the night I spent watchful hours that did not seem taken from sleep . . . I waited . . . Happily the moments which lend poignancy to waiting in Europe did not exist here. No twilight; no dawn. Night and day succeeded each other more rapidly than if they had been controlled by an electric button. When, prepared for melancholy I seated myself by the edge of the sea, drawing it gently toward me with a movement which must have uncovered, across the world, a little bit of Peru; when I sat facing the setting sun, waiting for all those artificial evening colors which in Bellac give the soul its true reflections, waiting for the lagoon to turn violet, the pearl fields orange, the trees purple, the sky vermillion, then hardly had the sun commenced to redden before a hand let it fall and there was no longer anything but night. A night which was always dazzling, milky, and which suddenly, at the end of twelve hours, restored me to a day that was instantly pompous and shining red. Ceaselessly I was emptied from this silver shell into this shell of gold. Complete night fell at the first call of melancholy. Full day arose at the first anguish. This obsidien, lacquered world welcomed grief no more than rain.

Soon, therefore, I forgot my sadness and left it alone to dispose itself in me like a tumor.

But it is time that I describe my island to you . . .

.   .   .   .

You are going to be disappointed. Not that it was not heaped with beautiful trees, and with minerals which serve as the standard by which all other minerals are judged,—which are to them what gold is to other metals,—and with butterflies by whose presence one judges a collection. But I could not tell you the names of these marvels. My education in equatorial flora and fauna had been neglected at Bellac. Without too much difficulty I identified the cocoanut trees and the birds of paradise, but that was all. In order to speak to you of plants I shall, therefore, employ incorrectly all the exotic words that I can recall: mangroves, mandrakes, and manchineels; all that grand opera taught me of botany. And in order to describe the most beautiful aviary in the world I shall use either very simple words—tricolored hen, bibbed magpie— or, so that the scenery may be in keeping, the three or four words which, at the age of ten, we derisively retained from a travel book dealing with Guinea, and which we used to nickname our playmates: ptemerops, goura Morandi, and Maucna.

All the birds of the Pacific came to land on my island which was laid out like the ground signal on an aerodrome: the outer border was in coral and pearl shell, the second belt was of cocoanut trees, the third of flowers and short grass; in the center were two hills set in virgin forest. The green zones shone during the day; the shell ring gleamed at night; exactly at noon two little lakes on the hill-tops were lit up. Thousands of unknown birds fluttered around me like a new language. The whole island was in a flurry at the slightest wind. Whenever I lifted my arm too suddenly it was as though I had shaken a red or blue carpet; and when I awoke and spread my arms to yawn it seemed as though I had unsewn this carpet. The west wind carried balls of down toward the sea and they floated on the lagoon like dummy swans until they reached a point where the current seized them and carried them compact, in pillows, toward the Kuro Sivo . . . I tried to orient myself in this aviary. The presence of some bird mentioned by Jules Verne or in my natural history classes would have informed me of my location in the world. I knew that the cassowary announces land which is near Australia, since it comes from Tasmania on foot; but I sought my cassowary in vain . . . that the

7

bustard indicates South Africa; but there was no
bustard . . . that the Equator may still harbor pre-
historic birds; and when I saw, spying at me from
behind a tree, a bald head with a beak like an old
horn, I was afraid, asking myself if it was not
upheld by a bristly reptilian neck, if it did not issue
from a hairy sparadrap body with webbed feet.
But this island was also a garden for the fashion-
able species, a style-shop for feathers. Everywhere
were birds of paradise and aigrettes, and little crows
pricked with marabout and ostrich feathers. Parrots were all around, appearing to hang from the
cocoanut trees by a thread, like the tassels of a curtain
cord. Still ignorant of human language, they only
repeated the cries of the first parrot, or they climbed
in groups of ten by their beaks, stopping in echelon
on the trunk like balls of blue, yellow and red resin.
The cockatoos who went to sleep in the second
island every evening were in a frenzy at meeting
the gouras who were coming from over there to
sleep in mine. From here and there came birds
whose photographs I had seen in the *Journal des
Voyages:* the one called the Mute-Bird, which always
alighted on the branch just above the singing bird,
opening its beak without emitting a sound; the one
called the Ugliest-in-the-World, whom I recog-

nized immediately as the ugliest, for he appeared
to have all the minor human maladies—so humiliating for tenors and young husbands. He had
corns on his feet, boils on his neck, a sty; and he
sneezed. He was however the first to become tame,
having, like all ugly men, a kindly heart. Red,
black, and golden sparrows which became colorless
balls when they alighted; blackbirds, which were a
dirty white while flying, and which became pears
of purple and indigo so soon as they settled. Sometimes I stumbled on a barn-yard travesty being
played out on the beach by vermillion geese, tricolored ducks, green and golden turkeys, carmine
peacocks; and at my slightest movement all these
colors changed as in a kaleidoscope. Roosters, hens
and guinea-hens, but under the protection of a
millionaire proprietor. Sometimes I found the tree
on which they were setting. It was beloved for
its horizontal branches on all of which were squatting females and upright males, all of them as
though stuffed upon a Christmas tree. The nearer
one approached the top the larger the species became and the more vivid their colors; and the nest
on the last branches could no longer contain the
tails of the paradise birds. At times a Mucuna
Benetti struck against me, or alighted on me, as

he had never seen a human being before. He would peck at me, confusing skin with bark. I felt that some of these birds would have loved to live upon me, being for a woman what they were for the crocodile or rhinoceros in other climes, won over by the gentleness of a large creature, asking only that they might announce the approach of my enemies. All of them were friendly, allowing themselves for the most part to be approached and caressed; and in this respect alone my adventure resembled a real dream.

Sometimes there were great councils among the various bird laborers, the weavers, the mowers, the sawers and sorters, the planters of reeds and the planter of shells, as though it were their ultimate intention to build a model communal nest. At evening, a flight of small pigeons sometimes lighted hastily on a mango tree, condemning the bats, who hung there in clusters throughout the day, to wander about until morning. In each tree a perpetual puss-in-the-corner game went on, causing hundreds of wings to flutter. At times there were trees so laden down that I plucked a large bird with my hand, like a ripe fruit, in order to save the branch. I tried to frighten the birds by shouts, whereupon they all turned toward me on their perches, looking at me. If I tried to frighten them by gesticulations they turned their backs to me, the widows and the birds of paradise making the tree burst into flower. Certain birds that I had thought were land dwellers fell suddenly like stones to the bottom of the lagoon. Great attacks against the flowering pepper trees were made by ptemerops whose breast feathers were thereafter puffed out with grains. All my movements, all my habitual actions had a punctual escort of colors: two blue parrots when I ate bananas; two bistre divers when I opened oysters; two orange wagtails when I gathered mangos. They always flew together, taking off and alighting at the same instant, always separated by the same distance, so that each of my glances might have its ray . . . During the first months this aviary saved me from solitude, for I took the tenderness of the feathers to indicate the tenderness of the birds themselves.

But, little by little, I was compelled to recognize that they and I did not belong to the same epoch in the world's history. I lacked vertebrates and mammals as companions of the flood. I grew tired of seeing unoccupied around me all those air-spaces which I had been taught from infancy lodged my slaves of burden: goats, dogs, and horses. At evening, on each limb, there were a thousand decapitated balls and only one bird with a round, visible ear keeping watch among so many headless bodies. Never any other companions. Never any companions with oblique eyes, with oval eyes, with eyelids; always those little cymbals which were covered at night with white leather. Never trickery, or tenderness, or intelligence: one felt that the first cat, the first mongoose had not yet been born. Never—as I have seen them with emotion in the country—were the bodies of the females distended gently little by little: the dogs with their little ones, the large cows with their udders, the bitches heavy with their litters. On this island life was transmitted, between creatures who remained forever thin, only by some jugglery, only by green and violet eggs speckled with brown. Never any gravid creatures; never even those little animals that we place like paperweights on fluttering sentiments; the weazle on malice; the ermine on gentleness. The turtles had disappeared a few days after my arrival, and as soon as the birds assembled on the shore, or aligned themselves on the creepers as on telegraph wires, I was afraid that they might all abandon me in an instant. I felt that they were at the mercy of the slightest breath which would announce—falsely per-

haps—winter or a typhoon. I had put two of them
in a cage, so that in case they all departed there
would remain with me at least two living companions. I changed them every day, and for some
hours they would be more excited and more lively,
as though it were merely their appearance and their
color that I had changed. This was, as a matter
of fact, practically useless: they all remained with
me, striking against an imaginary wall fifty metres
from the island. Migratory birds in mid-season,
mad like a compass needle placed on the Pole itself.
A giant gesture and every living thing on the island
save me, would have been swept away. I often
felt myself at the mercy of a sudden quarrel with
these uncomprehending birds, who, on the day that
I should inadvertently vex or frighten them, would
abandon their eggs and leave for other islands, without giving me a chance to justify myself. I was
gentle with each species, and mistrustful and sly,
as one is when he lives with an unknown god; flattering the Ugly-Bird with hypocritical phrases,
loudly complimenting the Mute upon his song. But,
without telling them, pretending that I was searching for some jewel, I sought for an animal in this
island with the same glance that one seeks a boat at
sea. And it came to pass that I discovered (it was

the best the Pacific could do for me; it was my
only child by it) a bird which had hair, a beak which
had teeth,—a fine ornithorhynchus.

.   .   .   .

It is not true that a ship passed one morning a
few miles off shore; it is not true that I had nothing
ready, neither search-light nor cloth, with which
to signal it. I saw three white bands on its funnel.
To-day I could hunt up the Line and find out the
names of those who came so close to me. I ran
gesticulating along the beach, stirring up great waves
of birds; mute, knowing how useless any cries of
mine would be. It was at the time when I still
wore a tunic: I waved it from the promontory, most
scandalous heroine. I undressed myself for men,
who at least did not see me.

It is not true that I thereafter wished to die of
hunger. That I stretched myself out in the water
so that I might drown as well. That I left my head
above the sea, against a stone, so that I might also
die of sunstroke. That I thought of all the vilest
and lowest things in the world so that I might die
of indignation in the bargain. That I opened all
around me every form of death, like gas-jets, and
waited. But all forms of death turned away, called
to richer tasks far from this lonely child. The sun

disappeared. The sea drew back. The whole sky
suddenly gave me news of Europe: large hairy stars
trembled against the night like the toy tin spiders
on the umbrella of the peddler near the Brasserie
Universelle . . . God promised me that I should
pass by there again, flanked by autobusses . . . God
promised me that some day I should buy toy spiders,
toy grasshoppers and explosive cigars for my children, in the store near the Madelaine . . . I was
saved . . .

It is not true that I spent my days in pumice-
stoning my limbs and in rubbing them with a pearl-
shell powder which made them veritable silver in the
sunlight. Soon it was my whole body. I no longer
had anything but a big hat or an umbrella. After
the few months during which the greatest optimist
insists on living like a shipwrecked person—always
on the beach, measuring trees with his eye as though
for future boats, persistently seeking hooks for
trout that let themselves be caught by hand, and
traps for birds that do not know how to escape you,
who alight on your shoulder as on your gun in
Europe—I renounced being anything other than
an idler and a millionaire. I stretched feather
screens from cocoanut tree to cocoanut tree, at times
fastening them for hours by living birds; for the

most beautiful feathers faded once they had fallen.
I had hundreds of enormous pearls procured by
diving, which, not knowing how to pierce them,
I wore on my neck and knees like tiny balls
in small net bags. I had perfumes of fresh resin
mixed with pollen; lotions obtained from my sugar-
tree. These were always too heady; but once I had
been soaked in the waters of the spring and then
dried by the sun I was certainly the best smelling
thing in the entire archipelago . . . I had my
eleven rice powders: one of pearl-shell which made
me shining; one which made me dull; one which
colored me red; and, dearest of all, the one that I
had put on for the perfect's ball at Limoges. And I
dried myself in the large leaves of a gray banana
tree as though in blotting-paper . . .

Sacrilegious European, I made for myself everything by which the Polynesians honor their dead.
I stretched myself out in those wooden houses in the
tree-tops in which their corpses decay, and when I
stirred I was a cause of astonishment in little spar-
row-hawks who had come from islands where people
did die. I coated myself with palm oil and mica,
and appeased myself with all those honors and attentions which are employed to appease phantoms.

If I peevishly neglected myself for a day my

make-up quickly peeled, and my slightest sorrow made me look as though I had come from an orgy. But that passed quickly. And at last there came the first evening when I calmly lay down to sleep in the centre of the island—instead of stretching myself out beside the sea parallel to one of its movements—at the exact centre of the island, sacrificing through indolence half my chances of rescue . . .

It is not true that I embraced the ornithorhynchus, that I rummaged in his little pocket and found nothing there, no forgotten letter. He complained softly with cries like a duck. It is not true that I scratched the swelling near his skull. He wagged his tail like a dog. It is untrue that I stuffed him with little eggs. He clapped his paws together in front of him like a beaver.

.   .   .   .

Every day, now, I swam around the island until I reached the point from which I had to cross its full width in order to return to the promontory. Before I had cleared the belts of sand and of coral I was already dry. Then came the cocoanut trees and five minutes of shade. I made a detour for the sake of placing my hand, with its five fingers spread wide, in the five little branches which came from a single limb, and which were so formed as to make

one believe they were a hand with large and small
joints. For by this time I had taken an inventory
of everything in the island which resembled a creature of my own species . . .

Then came the plain, cut by three streams; the
sectors alternated between turf and *catelyas*, and
were sown with fields of sunflowers similar to our
Jerusalem artichokes. On these flowers the parrots
pastured, the greediest flinging themselves forward
with outspread wings, trying to eat the suns themselves. All the colors of the rainbow, each with
its cry, confounded around a single yellow disk.
Then, having passed around the *balivier* which had
been struck by lightening and which resembled the
statue of a man, a man almost; after crossing little
marshes, cut out of coral, from which rose orchids
ten metres high, like fountains, with a bird circling
above them instead of above an egg; there came a
kind of meadow where my steps were muffled,
where the birds kept silent, where the innumerable
flowers were without perfume, which provoked in
me—so naked and so powdered with pearl—a feeling of non-existence, or the impression of a field in
hell. Noiseless and almost motionless battles between animals that should have been brought together by no power, not even hate: humming-birds

disputing with spiders; little geese with their beaks
caught between the lips of giant frogs; palm tree
crabs held in the coils of adders.

It was close by that a hip came forth from a sleek
tree trunk—a complete woman's hip, always in the
sunlight, warm as if the metamorphosis had just
been accomplished—and I caressed it with some
little curiosity as though there had just occurred in
this place the accident that changes one into a tree:
an attack by lascivious gods, or an access of over-
weening pride.   This also was the spot where the
noise of the cascades equalled the noise of the sea upon the reefs, where the forest opened in a thousand
golden passages like a honey-comb.   Unconsciously
I entered the one from which I had seen the largest
bird come forth.   The *catleyas* on which I walked
were four or five times bigger than in Europe and
were soft and brittle under my feet like mushrooms.
I hurried, following a wistaria creeper which led
me to glades of jasmine and holly-hocks where I
inhaled with all my breath perfumes violent enough
to kill, as though they were merely air.   Each glade
was a cemetery: there, a tree at whose foot lay the
bodies of enormous shrikes; there, a circle of turf
on which turtles, after a thousand years of travel
from one pole to the other, had ended their lives.

There were dozens of these, only their shells remaining; all exactly the same size, all dead at exactly the same age. The eye, the real human eye which was fitted in the manchineel-tree, with its iris pierced my me, contemplated all this . . . At last the central glade, with little sleeping eagles decorated with two spots on their shoulders, resembling scarabs; where sombre peacocks preserved with difficulty around their necks a few of the live embers which would inundate all the peacocks of my island in the spring . . . where stood the rock from which fell lichens like the tresses of a woman's hair . . . where bits of rotted wood lay at my feet, resembling jawbones, Arcadian superciliaries, human elbows . . .

All this was not merely imagination. I have since seen the names given by scientists to these human forms: the wooden eye was aptly named *nodus oculus* by Littré; Buffon called the lichen *capilla Irenei;* and the two sleek, bent over trunks on which I was going to sit down, twining my arms around the high trunk, Blaringhem has denominated *osculus Rodini* . . . It was from this spot that I saw the paradise birds hurling themselves through the forest like torches exchanged by jugglers . . .

.   .   .   .

Such was my over brilliant island, with days when the mother of pearl and the shells were made according to Brasso and Faineuf; sometimes trembling with little earthquakes when one coral pressed ahead more swiftly than his mates or when three madrepores quarreled. All these colors, all these giant *catleyas* drank up my solitude and my sorrow like blotting paper. So that I often seemed to myself not strayed but dead. It seemed that I had commenced the migration which takes you from star to star while transforming your molecules. On a star of the thousandth magnitude, of four or five kilometres, I had become a girl-bird. Already I had caught myself putting my head under my arm in order to sleep, and there remained to me scarcely any other human contradiction than that I felt during the day that I was a sister of the night birds, and during the night that I was the sister of the day birds.

CHAPTER V

AFTER rejoicing in this island innocence I was disappointed in it. I had less respect for nature: I experimented on her, in order to provoke or insult her, with all the actions which would have cost me dear in France which is called innocent. I tasted the berries which resembled our poisonous berries; I stuffed myself with belladona and fried hemlock, sure that they contained only a harmless and pleasant sugar. I slept in the shade of walnut trees; I tasted large scarlet mushrooms: in France I would have had spotted fever, numb fingers, twitching eyelids; but solitude vaccinated me against all these ills. It was tiresome to see those naive palm trees on which only a crab climbed up and down, following the sun, like the weight of a pendulum; those large sharp leaves into which I plunged my arm and which never closed on it; never a flower which tried to bite or hold even my little finger; those clumps of heliotrope, those bunches of sunflowers which moved their heads slowly in unison toward the sun like chorus girls; those parrots which applauded at my slightest word; those echos; those birds of paradise, familiar as in paradise itself; those gouras which remained calmly on their branch even when I shouted, deigning at most, through politeness, to lift themselves as high as one lifts a hat (leaving maddened on the instant an echo reached them which was imperceptible to me); this nature, in sum, which did not keep its distance with a human being, which was paralyzed by happiness, by the impossibility of bringing conduits of poison from the mainland; this nature whose reflexes—the flight of birds, the retreat of lizards—never functioned even when struck at the proper spot, at times exasperated me. Never a ray of sunlight cut by a cloud, or suddenly vanishing: all of them were soaked in the ocean or the earth, held by a sleeping fisherman who never pulled them up. Never a fish which fled from you—for neither the sun nor the sea had their reflexes—and it was necessary to tickle the trout in order to draw from them some vague reverence. Perhaps a man could have obtained more of a reaction from this island which was placid beneath me like a horse under a woman rider.

However I was becoming a stronger and more agile creature: I climbed, I swam, and little round

8

balls, muscles, glided under my skin at every movement.   But in order to make the birds afraid or to
enslave the trees ten years, at least, of fire or mas-
sacre would have been necessary.   All those liquorice
roots, all those foolish vanilla grasses, those trunks
which were milk and those stones which were pearls,
would have required at least one human couple to
transform them into bits of sterile wood and tares
as in Europe.   My heart, too, had become inoffensive . . . the island had slipped between it and
the world like putty.   Nothing made it beat any
more.   I was in such good training that it no longer
accelerated even when I ran or when I swam.
Sometimes I tried to link myself, from a distance,
with the sorrow, the unhappiness, and the tears
which seasons and cities distribute in the country
under an unfailing pressure.   In my desire to
suffer I went to look for last memories preceding
my shipwreck, as above a spot where one picks up a
cable. I tried to persuade myself that I was informed
by telepathy, by winks and by shivers, of the evils
which had befallen Europe and the death of my
friends.   It was useless.   During the space of a
year I was able to weep only once, and that by
chance, when I thought of a broach (coral of course;
the first sliver I ever saw of that material on which

I would have to live) which was the first present
ever given me, which I had lost in a fountain and
which had made me hate for a whole evening everyone who had not dived in after it. For so little did I
anticipate that it would subsequently expand in the
ocean and save me.

.   .   .   .

Happily, also, the island had need of me at this
time. For some days the current which circled the
reefs, and then pierced the lagoon in order to graze
the headland, had been carrying bunches of leaves and
islets of interlaced trees; sometimes half falling over,
sometimes upright, as in pictures of the Mississippi.
There were large flowers on them . . . Perhaps the
wind could not carry off their pollen, or perhaps they
belonged to those species which nature has to trans-
port bodily to other plants and other islands,—plants
which love after the fashion of men. But from the
largest I saw a creeper detach itself, swim, come
alongside a bush and twist itself around it: a
boa-constrictor. I killed it in its sleep the same
evening, but not before it had eaten two gouras . . .
A week later I was fearfully revictualed from above,
as a besieged garrison is by aviators: a hawk, before
being touched by my sling-shot, had time to taste a
specimen of all my birds. Then, on one of those

derivitive islets, I thought I saw a hairy animal, an
ocelot or a cougar, which I kept from throwing
himself upon me by threatening him along the beach
with a flaming branch. . . .

I was touched by dangers which were at last
abroad upon my island. Providence had requisi-
tioned from Bellac what was, perhaps, the one attack
that could injure it. My heart had jumped three
times, like the hearts of those who are falling in love
. . . One day I discovered an alligator twenty centimetres long: I knew that it would be many years before he would become dangerous—ten years at least
before he could successfully eat the ornithorhynchus,
twenty years before it could seize a wading-bird by
its foot. For the time being I kept him in a basin.
Then he disappeared and there was no more theoriz-
ing, even at ten years' distance, regarding my animal
or my hand, or—even at twenty years'—regarding
my birds.

. . . .

Alone? . . . Not completely . . . The personages whom we had invented at the convent—the one
who slammed the shutters, who stirred the forest,
whom we called the Novice; and the one who broke
the plates and dishes, who caught his feet in strings,
who overturned tubs at midnight in sleeping cot-

tages, whom my cousins had named the Controler, after the clumsiest functionary in Limoges—these two, faithful across Atlantic and Pacific, made a point of rejoining me. One day I was awakened from my siesta by sheet-iron falling from a roof.

"The Controler!"

For a whole week, in fact, the Controler lorded it on the island; but he quickly saw the way of things and this first inexplicable sound was the only European noise to which he resorted. But cocoanuts fell accurately on crabs and crushed them. I found a turtle with a broken shell, birds caught in creepers: he had passed that way . . . Then one day two little clouds left the west and went to install themselves in the east with enough dignity for a quadrille. The wind began to blow, and the Controler turned things over to the Novice. Trees were shaken to their roots and from every hole appeared clouds of birds. The Novice took the same liberties with the banana and palm trees that he had allowed himself in Limousin with leaves, branches and foliage . . . Only the birds with short plumage dared to alight at random: the tails of the paradise birds and the widows were blown over their heads in a squall at their slightest false move. The Novice tried on me, naked, all the pleasantries which he allowed himself with my dresses

in Bellac.   And many others visited me after this:
those whom the boarding school girls called the
Architect, Coco or Casmir, who peeled entire bunches
of bananas in a second, who changed the maple
syrup into glue, who caused to reappear on me, by
inexplicable red marks, the traces of garters, corset,
or shoulder-straps . . . some whose names I did not
know.   A real savage would have made them gods,
so lively was their malice.   A thousand breaths, a
thousand little disturbances, a thousand small pres-
ences, which moved around me, begging for that
divinity which they knew from the books of Spencer
is easier to obtain in Polynesia than elsewhere in
the world.   I was assailed by their ambitions.   I
instinctively understood them.   A rustling in the
catleyas just at sunrise wished to be god of the red
ray.   A flash on the sun-flowers wished to be goddess
of the green ray.   A wail in the forest pleaded, de-
manded in a voice that was almost human, that it
might be the god of silence.   A bellowing from the
big orchids, as from a phonograph, for the place
of pollen gods . . .   Whenever I passed beneath the
tree with the inverted roots I received a sharp, brutal
blow on my shoulder, perhaps from the one who
wished to become god of caresses.   A limitless ambition in the least reflections in the water and in the

springs possessed isolated fishes who were suddenly
rigid and ridiculous. The half-calls, the half-flashes,
of modest ones who wished to be only demi-gods.
A unanimous flattery which was calculated to make
me believe myself of royal blood, so that all of them
under my protection might hurl themselves upon the
quarry of nobility. A very round cloud which
paraded before me every day toward noon, painted
and powdered, like Esther before her king, with the
secret pretention of having a rank among the cumuli;
the rock-breakers around the island who, with their
noise of fire wished to make of me an awakened
Valkyrie; the sea that sometimes slid away from the
horizon like a cake from its mold, that I would have
created a goddess at such moments to have it return.
I refused to make good these infantile vows. Only
the Novice and the Controller preserved an official
existence in the midst of their Pacific rivals. I turned
away from the cloud, from the ray, in the mood of
a prince who is being solicited. I guarded against
certain gestures as if they would, in themselves,
confer titles on all these demons; as sometimes happens when the King of Spain puts on his hat or
uses *thou*. I said *you* to the birds, to the island. I
mistrusted even myself, knowing that women create
from themselves, and even without child-birth,

beings greater than they. I did not wish to give
any fear, any hope, any perfume on the island the
right of calling itself my equal. Often, at evening,
when all the unchained forces of the wind, the sea,
and the archipelago assailed me; when I heard them
begging, confused despite everything like a mother
who has not given names to her numerous children;
when, little and eternal, they discovered me under
my feathers and my leaves and pulled on me like
the ring of a trap-door that would open everything
to them; when I stood up in the midst of their jubila-
tion; when they fanned me, caressing me in all the
recesses of my soul, touching my body with real
hands, caressing the lining of my skin and the inside
of my eyes, seeing in this girl from France their
one chance of ever achieving divinity; and when
perfumes mingled, and the odor of wistaria became
so strong that I wrinkled my eyebrows as one does
in Europe when the gas is left on; and when each
future demon, thinking to tempt me, let me choose
him, even to his sex, letting me decide the kind of
love he would enjoy; when it would have sufficed
for me to wink my eye in order to bestow upon
them that liberty which I alone, for a thousand
leagues around, could bestow; when, in the midst of
their already familiar voices, I heard the cry of a

new colleague come from the ends of Oceania, having learned of my presence; when they beseiged me,
disdaining some real Polynesian queen in a neighboring island because they knew that I, who had been
educated at Savageon, was richer in magic words
and illustrious names, better fed with poems and
glories, and because they suddenly desired a European title; when I chased the wind away with my
hand as one chases an insect at home or chased the
sea with my foot, like a dog (foolish sea which
offered itself utterly at this moment for the sake of
changing its terrible common name for a little caressing word); when I said to them: you need not tell
me that you are Aeolus, that you are Orpheus; you
are only the wind, you are only the *catleya,* you are
only the sea; and when the sun and the moon, above
such vanities, with their names of Apollo and Diana
stuck on them like the name on a station, approved
of me; then, at times (must I confess it?) a regret
seized me at not being as greedy as they, a desire to
sacrifice to my eternity a few of the treasures that
were in me, a desire to select for myself from all
the many marvellous words at my service the hundred which were most beautiful, and, in defiance of
all these anonymous demons, to cover my hands, my
knees, and even my thoughts with divine appellations.

I would succumb for a moment to this crown that was offered me. Despite myself I was more formal, I walked with a more noble step on this island; I forced my glance to be more brilliant, more dominating. Quite naked, I went as with a train. Already artful as a false god, knowing the habits of the stars and the elements, like children who count three in order to make a train start, I said "Go to bed," to the sun, in the presence of my wonderstruck demons, when the sun touched the horizon. But the hierarchical sentiment is the strongest in the Latin soul. The sudden thought of those people in Europe who I felt were my true masters; those tram conductors who misdirect you; those travel bureaus which martyrize you; those coachmen who enclose you in smelly boxes; those taxis, refuges, and platforms where I had always been, and would be after my return, nothing but a paying slave, cheered me and robbed me of any pretention, even a secret one, of being a god. I came out from the ray in which, despite myself, I had been lodged, as from a disguise.

The months passed. I had quickly learned to calculate by the moons. I rejoiced over a full moon as one does over a salary at home: I was happy that my eyes had rolled this ball to its maturity. But

already I felt cramped by these small divisions of
time.   I still obeyed the quarterly desire for vaga-
bondage which had formerly pushed me to tailors
and dressmakers.   I now desired seasons; but I did
not succeed in discovering any.   There was nothing
in the island by which I could any longer distinguish
an autumn or a winter.   At times a red fringe on the
leaves of one tree would appear to indicate a late
spring or the close of summer; but the neighboring
tree would only be greener.   Sometimes the moon
was thin and transparent, one saw stars through it
as in summer; but the sun was not a degree stronger,
and here the two did not live at each other's expense.
An entire year had been placed at the foot of each
bush for it to consume slowly according to its fancy.
I believed I had discovered that a kind of lime-tree
lost its foliage.   I was delighted.   So at last I would
see shoots thrust out, branches grow green.   I came
every day to gather each leaf, and set fire to a heap
of them with the magnifying glass which always
made me see the object that I was going to destroy
two or three times its natural size: in an instant I
could see a dead leaf, an autumn, three times larger
than in Europe . . .   But soon I understand my
mistake: the tree was dead forever.   No seasons.
I spent entire hours searching for traces of them, in

the hills, in the grass.   One moment I found a false
spring, thanks to a thousand fresh green perroquets
on a grove.   For a whole night I was deceived by a
false winter, thanks to the false mother of pearl frost
. . .   And I lost my way in my walks and rambles
as though I had been robbed of the four points of
the compass along with the four seasons.

Now I was awakened one morning by the cries
of unknown birds.   The whole island was in an uproar.   I sought to see these new guests who had just
alighted in their myriads around me.   But I could
distinguish only the same gouras, the same sparrows,
and the same adjutants, motionless on their branches
or in their accustomed places.   Complete nightingale
improvisations, the songs of black-birds and canaries;
but I tried in vain to catch sight of the singers.   At
last I understood . . .   These cries came from my
birds.   Each one of these myriad songsters was
lodged in one of my mute companions.   That conch-
like whistle issued from pigeons who habitually
clucked.   Those black-bird notes came from the
aigretted young lady who hitherto had spoken only
in sneering laughs.   The paradise birds with vocal
chords of zinc were suddenly softened and modu-
lated.   Either I was witnessing a miracle, or I saw
the untying of a chord in the throats and hearts· of

these birds, including the ptemerops who uttered an accordion-like noise.   Or indeed (but how much greater a miracle!) it was spring . . .

I was on one knee, on the watch for my season. The light was so clear that a gnat in it looked like a bubble in a pane of glass.   But the birds were taking care of the gnats!   The sunlight was at once a half-degree warmer and fresher, and the gnat, full of adventure, let the island fall like ballast, and flew directly toward the sun!   The birds, feeling the grass grow and the branches creak with sap, refused to alight; each of them hovering over what was going to be a new bud.   The languid bustards sat on the Ranunculus bulbs as though they were eggs.   Youth.alighted on the corals, the parrots and the baobabs.   In my thought the word *young* was added to every word as an open car is added in springtime to every tram in Europe; the young millinarian ocean; the young old cockatoos: I felt my chagrin and my despair becoming young and strong within me.   In a paler blue one recognised the deepest vasts of heaven.   Hope was attached to the tail of each bird, like the twisted papers school children stick to the feet of flies.   The water of my most placid stream was suddenly frisky and cold like mountain water.   In a single night the turtles' shells and the lizards' hides were more brightly polished than combs and pocketbooks, and were girdled, too, with gold and silver. Everything from which spring is made in France—snow, masses of ice,—seemed to be hidden in a storehouse in the center of the island. A green afflux started from the stems of the banana leaves and pushed the yellow sap toward the end of the leaf, like the real color in dyed hair, but at a pace sensible to the naked eye. On all the trees all the insects climbed straight like lady-bugs. Carabids, luminous at night, fluttered in full sunlight like lanterns that no one has remembered to extinguish on the morning following a lawn party; but their little flame was the only obscure thing. The leaves of the palm trees opened, cracking like the hands of a skeleton coming to life. The fish, sensing the cloak of youth that had fallen on the sea, tore it, with their dorsal fins completely out of water. In the breaking waves one could see schools of herring touch the air itself with their silvery flanks. And then suddenly, supreme proof— from what bird did this cry come; from some Numidian crane; from some humming-bird; from some king-fisher; from some adjutant?—I heard the cuckoo!

Spring lasted for three days. Three days when

plants and birds were in a frenzy. The leaves of all
the cocoanut trees and mangroves, all the limbs, were
lifted up, and I could no longer find shade beneath
them.   Below these upturned branches the birds
seemed more naked and more sensitive. The creepers
came together in an embrace that had been loosened a
centimetre by the year just passed. For the first time
the humming-birds flew in pairs, the male indicating
forbidden perfumes.   Under the thicket were big
splotches of vivid yellow sunlight, the tails of cocks
who were fighting. At times I stood stock still, halted
by one of those white threads which bar our orchards
in May, determined to remain caught in this European net.   Then, on the evening of the third day, all
the paradise birds engaged in a battle: only one of
them, the weakest and the smallest was killed; and,
as though it had been satisfied by the slightest prey
on the island, spring disappeared. The flowers were
already losing their brilliancy, like the feathers of
a killed bird. I would be lucky to have three days
of winter before the coming of the next spring!

.   .   .   .

Other months passed. The one when I was bitten
by a fish, the one when I cut my finger; and they
left their notches on me. I now had the same ac-

quaintance and knowledge of pure waters and fruits that one acquires in Europe of wines and cookery. There was one spring which I preferred; I knew my best banana tree, my best mango. Perhaps I still confused the things which one can not distinguish without a diploma: I was ill, and I thought myself sad; I shivered with fever, and I thought that I was cold. Suddenly I felt unsuspected springs of my soul burst forth like whale-bones from a worn out material, revealing to me my true qualities. In this way I discovered one day that I was brave, as something cracked within me. Thenceforward I renounced fear. Another day I felt ashamed of myself, for I no longer smiled; I was without vivacity and utterly dull, abandoning my powders and my unguents: I taunted myself; I repeated to myself that I was not, after all, either a Russian or a German that I should take my life so tragically. I had to play the part of a Frenchwoman alone on an island; when I caught my foot in a creeper I had to beg a thousand pardons of the creepers. I decided that one day a week, at sunrise or at sunset, whatever the time, I would be gay. I even fixed the first appointment for the following day, and in agony I awaited this interview with my old time gaiety like a meeting with a stranger . . . A long night, visited

by all those shadows which throw themselves upon
dimly lighted hearts . . . But at the end of it I
felt a smile spread over my face. Without argument
the sun rose from the sea . . . I awoke beside the
perfumed cocoa-trees as I had formerly awakened
beside my chocolate . . . I smiled, my eyes
wrinkled, my cheeks dimpled: gaiety hung from
my face by a thousand clips, like a piece of linen
about to flutter . . . But it was not my gaiety alone
which returned to me: there came with it a modesty
that I no longer knew. Never did an American
or Italian woman, alone on an island, contemplate
her body, her own body, in the unique mirror of a
magnifying glass, with more happy embarrassment.
A mango that I squeezed too hard burst and drenched
me. Never did a Cuban or Liminien woman, never
did a naked Oriental, receive on herself the juice of
a broken mango with more blushes . . . And, until
midday, I addressed to the rising sun all the coquet-
ries of which a Frenchwoman, dressed in red feathers,
is capable . . . So it was that nothing within me
obeyed commands any longer. I found an unknown
variety of innocence when I was seeking gaiety; and,
the following week, in seeking piety, I discovered
some unfamiliar architectural enthusiasm which made
me move trees, weave creepers. Later I was possessed

9

by a passion for painting which led me to discover
the three or four sensitive spots in this shining ex-
panse which it was necessary to pierce, from which
particular colors really gave themselves to men: a
shell-fish which gave vermillion, a flower which
gave blue, and a little quarry which gave white-lead.
For the island felt obliged to secrete only French
resin, which I used only to accentuate all those
human appearances, of which I have told you, to
underline with violet the eyes in bark, to tint with
white the branches which resembled arms.   And
these colors kept the worms, caterpillars and
insects away from the manchineel-hips and the
palm-necks.   So all the roads by which thought
might win to a human body had their signs . . .
Poor companion, scattered in the living wood; eyes,
mouths, and lips elbowed about by vegetable sap . . .
sole companion! . . .

        .   .   .   .

It must have been a year after my shipwreck that
I was finally able to leave for the island opposite.
I had become a strong swimmer, and I had made
many starts before, but the current had always carried me back to the beach. One day I discovered that
the said current, after having made the turn of my

island, swung off anew toward the other island.   It
was an easy route, and besides it was indicated by
the flocks of birds that followed the fishes.   I left
curiously but without hope.   I had quickly guessed
that the smoke which rose over there came from a
hot spring as on my own island.   I merely felt that
I was changing from one scale to another in a balance, for the sake of verifying some unknown weight
of my own.   I started out.   In the case of my own
body I could not escape all the annoying delays which
attend the launching of a great boat.   One day I
caught a cramp and had to turn back.   The next day
I cut my feet on a reef and had to wait for them to
heal.   At last, on a morning when the current was
marked out with sleeping birds like buoys, and the
sea was opaline, like *eau de Cologne* into which one
has poured water, too much water, I departed, escorted toward the deep by my favorite birds.   Like
a porter who absents himself for a moment, I had
written on a board conspicuously placed near my
cave—in English and in French, like an educated
porter—"I am in the other island, I am coming
back. . ."

CHAPTER VI

IT was an easy voyage. To speak like the pro-
testants in their tales of shipwreck: God caused
a great fish, which I mistook for a torpedo, to strike
me without exploding. God caused me to cut
through councils of beautiful ablets, disposed in tiers,
and immovable, like the elect in the paintings of
Tintoretto. God (not without having filled my
mouth on two separate occasions with his great salt
humor) caused me to discover a passage through the
reefs, to find footing in a lagoon, my head thrust
forward; and suddenly, as though God finally opened
those ears which for a whole year had been condemned to hear the song of birds but once, God
immediately abandoned me to clamors, yelpings,
whistlings, and barkings. Then God—while I shook,
and emptied with my little finger, my ears which
were full of water—caused mewings, neighings and
trumpetings. I was welcomed by all the cries of the
noisiest animals; that of the hippopotamus, that of
the cat, that of the onager, and unknown cries which
must have been those of the giraffe or the yak.

But they came from the tree-tops. I was disconcerted to find so little harmony, on the first occasion that she deigned to speak to me, in the voice of nature. I was like a deaf person whose cure is effected one day at a concert when the orchestra is breaking into a dada symphony. All the cocoanut trees were pealing forth like the pipes of an organ.

"Oh! Oh!" I cried. . . But I had already guessed. I was not afraid.

At my voice the orchestra fell silent. All the birds of the island flew away taking shelter behind me, recognizing the queen of birds whose presence divides the flying species from the invisible species. But, at the extreme tops of the trees, a whole ventriloquil fauna of rhinoceroses and zebras resumed its uproar. I raised my arms, and, as though this gesture of surrender were here a declaration of war, I was immediately bombarded with cocoanuts, bananas, hazel-nuts, and samples of everything that I might ever eat on this new island. But I could not see a single monkey. I did not go far from the shore, remaining ready to dive back into the sea should they prove too large a race. The greediest and the least patriotic among the monkeys, instead of sending me full nuts and bananas, sent me shells and skins which fluttered down. Then I heard the

cry of a beaten child, and I saw, tumbling from
creeper to creeper, none of which could support him,
a ridiculous monkey scarcely larger than a hurdy-
gurdy monkey (the last one of this height that I had
seen had been dressed). He turned to face me, but
he was unable to maintain even this balance, and I
suddenly saw his blue behind. All the others, indignant at the simultaneous betrayal of their presence
and their secret, took flight, and the green leaves
were perforated by a hundred indigo spots. I saw
them leap from tree to tree, come up from each tree
like a chimney-sweep, pursue each other like accusers,
and disappear. Then, a little farther off, I heard
them give vent to the same clamor, an exclamation
surely provoked by some other beast, but unanimous
this time, its accord witnessing the passage of a
creature which did not call forth from the monkeys
conflicting information and cries, as did a young
Bellac girl. . . A boa perhaps, or a wild beast. . .
But I was not afraid: I went forward. . . .

What joy for one who no longer knows what an
eye is, an eye without a white sheath, an eye other
than the eyes of birds, an eye, in fine, unstitched by
the real knife—for one who had sought for weeks a
fish with oval eyes—to see at every moment, born
from an instant of silence, a new little animal,—a

pair of eyes! Rats which leaped into the sea, falsely announcing that the island was going to founder. Guinea-pigs. Shrew-mice. I followed them with a glance that was astonished at not being raised, accustomed by birds to a vertical life which I had left behind that morning. . . I went along the sand, the part of the island on which I had the best chance of finding a human foot-print, seeking to distinguish it among the thousands of monkey tracks with the patience of a person hunting a four-leaf clover in a clover field. . . I could still hear the monkeys in the distance, again discordant: they were thinking of me. . . Then, after passing through the belt of cocoanut trees, I entered a high grassy spot planted with clumps of rose bushes. They were all dead: men had been there before. And everywhere there were gliding creatures, in place of those stupid colored spots which had accompanied me yesterday; and soon—watching me with that look by which he had won my confidence in childhood, lowering those ears which had conquered my tenderness, wiggling that nose which had made me love him—a rabbit. . .

Everywhere were the two eyes of a little actor, looking at me through an animal, through the decorations of my former existence: an antelope, a cat, or a martin. Everywhere, instead of the noise of

feathers, was the noise of steps, of trotting, of gallop-
ing; a European rhythm which restored to me slow-
ness and speed. At each instant beautiful red and
green birds rose straight up from under my feet, like
Italian rockets that are fired to distract a criminal
from his crime, a savant from his work; but I no
longer raised my eyes. I struck my foot against
big orange eggs, placed in my path to hinder my
pursuit of a hare or a badger: but I no longer gathered them. My whole day was spent in reversing
a movie of my childhood, which restored to me
guinea-pigs and squirrels. When I heard the rustling of grass, when a bush waved, I no longer had to
think, as on my island: "it is the east wind; it is the
west wind. . ." From my memory, scraping it
gently as though it had quills, a new animal escaped:
—"It is a peccary," I said to myself. . . . "It is an
iguana. . . It is, perhaps, an armadillo. . ." Every
insect, every plant gave to me, as to a creator, the
picture, the expectation, of the animal which lived
on it. Cockroaches? My mongoose was not far
off. . . Bees? Watch out for little bears. . .
Golden carabids? I was going to see a carabid
eater. From a shipwrecked soul, from a waif, I was
promoted to Alice in Wonderland. Still more than
she I experienced that internal delirium which is

provoked by the idea of a blue monkey, and that pity
for human suffering which an armadillo gives, and
that patriotic devotion which is a gift from a little
gray antelope, and that love of wise men and poets
that is given by the striped antelope. Each clod which
fell from the island into the sea became a muskrat
or an otter, and, regaining the island immediately,
compensated it in life and hide for all that it had
lost of rock and leaves. Still another movement of
the island and I would see the roots that were
plunged in the water move and become elephant
trunks, the tree-trunk speckled with age become the
neck of a giraffe. Then, as if the fruits were alive,
from among twenty fruits which I shook from a tree
a squirrel fell upon my shoulder. Already he had slid
down the length of my body: I had caught only a
squashed prune, but at least I had been grazed by
something other than a wing or a scale, by one of
those creatures that give more to men than hats or
combs, by one of those creatures destined to ornament not our heads but our bodies, by a creature of
my own temperature.

I realized now that had I encountered man
directly, without an intermediate stage, it would have
been too violent, too dangerous. . . But a beautiful sun, European search-light, was shining today on

these animals, with their little faults and little virtues, restoring to me only a sweet and childish
humanity. All the animals of fable were there; the
animals, which—when, at the age ten, I had believed
all human beings to be faultless—had made me believe in evil, in lightness, in egotism: there were the
same rabbits, rats, and weasels. I was once more in
a country where my mind and my heart had formerly
coined themselves and had passed current. What
use was there in being good among torpedo fish and
rainbow trout? To be obstinate with ptemerops and
gouras? To be voluptous with paradise birds and
hens? Here I felt, at this moment, that my every
movement, observed by a thousand eyes, caused some
heart to beat and made me a goddess in the brain of
some antelope or shrew-mouse. I no longer refused
over all these hides the royalty that I had disdained
over monsoons and coral. Then a doe passed me, with
a lame leg that was badly set at the fracture; but it
was fastened with a tarred bandage, and, as though
I had recognised the passage of a man from a graft
on a tree, I felt myself—the wildcat that appeared
suddenly, opening his jaws and spitting at me, added
somewhat to this feeling—inundated with tenderness. . .

It was certainly European tenderness, which includes caressing a living animal; never that of Asia which is to kill oneself for one's leader; never the American variety which is to pretend, in order to amuse one's partner, while dancing, that one has caught one's foot in some chewing-gum which has fallen to the floor. I tried to catch hold of one of these thousand animals. But those which were most familiar to my heart fled the fastest, and after an hour of running I had caught nothing but an armadillo. I did not know what to do with it, and it waited stupidly, as when you have been led to catch a passing stranger at blind-man's-buff. In default of touching the animals themselves, I tried to touch their little ones, to find a nest of wildcats, of foxes, of badgers: in vain. An opossum passed that I was unable to dig up. The monkeys continued their uproar, making a circuit of the island, rioting now and again,—reminiscent of the fanfares which are accorded distinguished citizens in towns on the first of January. Sometimes a creaking noise informed me that they were above me, silent and motionless until one of them fell, obliged to come down almost to earth to recover his simian adroitness. Then they beat a deafening retreat. . . But already a she-monkey was following me, attracted by the completely peeled bananas and whole slices of cocoanut with which I sowed my path. I suddenly turned around to face her, and instead of taking flight she rolled over on her back and with three feet—the lame one held aside from his honor—she held out her child toward me. It cried, but it did not resist. It made faces at me, but it embraced me. It struck me, but already it was looking over my shoulder as a rampart, and at the first rocking movement that I made it fell asleep while making a move to escape from me.

.   .   .   .

I had indeed re-entered life, for my following day, instead of being composed of interchangeable hours, parceled itself into episodes as in Europe. There was the episode of the earthquake, the episode of the she-monkey's death, the episode of the treasure.

Day was already reborn. The leaves of the banana tree, heaped with dew, capsized one after the other. This was the water that I loved to drink each morning, after having pressed a shaddock over the leaf itself. The metallic sound which my island sometimes gave forth was even more noticeable here. Saws grated; the palm trees struck together with a noise like zinc. Surrounded by the cries of monkeys —who played out by themselves all the fables of La Fontaine: meeting each other face to face on a creeper, and never yielding; pulling a she-monkey, who clutched a nut, along on her back by the tail; one below speaking to another above who was eating a banana—I had the sensation, more strongly than ever, of awakening in a public garden, not far from a factory. A mongoose passed at a gallop, and I was as startled as one is in the Jardin des Plantes when a mongoose escapes, my glance instinctively seeking some keeper. . . Whenever I stood up or lay down my little monkey slid from my shoulder to my chest, like the drop of water in a level. . . On the sea I saw those white-caps and those flakes (pride of housemaids) which apartments yield up in the morning. Above the invisible scaffoldings which the monkeys were tirelessly raising in front of the cocoanut trees in order to re-paint an invisible façade—clamoring when an invisible plank fell and was caught in the net which the martins and hedge-hogs traced around me—the humming-birds struck at hawk-moths which retarded their helicopters and then soared heavenward again . . . the whole island working for me like a workshop . . . it is then that the earthquake occurred. . .

At evening when everything was calm; when I was no longer ignorant, having lost sight of them, of one of the island's animals; when the monkeys, attracted by the moon, leaned from a tree over the sea, yelping when a pale monkey held his hand out from the water toward the boldest among them; when the kneeling antelopes went exhausted to sleep; when the squirrel families, chased from the tree-trunks, still ran about, finally going to bed with the birds; when the sea, which had been shaken and beaten all day long, was seized at the four corners and stretched to the breaking point; when the fountain from the hot spring dropped lower little by little; at the hour, in short, when I would have been expelled from this public garden,—then the she-monkey died.

Then this hostile island—whose terrible little jerks had not succeeded in unhorsing me, hanging as I was to all its wither-bands, its creepers and its roots—wished to take its revenge by humiliating me on the following day, by showing me a burlesque of two great human plays, played by grotesque animals: Love with armadillos; Death with a she-monkey. In the middle of a round glade for Love, on an open bank for Death, with all the precautions for clarity and evidence that nature takes when she wishes to win a academician to materialism, I saw the armadillos make love, the she-monkey die. But at least the monkey, like a great actress, portrayed what is in Europe the death of a day-old friend. Friends of a day's standing who die at evening mentally link their death and your meeting, think that they die from the latter, and pardon you. They point with their finger to the spot where they are suffering. They accept the banana with enthusiasm, they let it fall with a shiver of disgust, and they kiss your hand. . . With a glance they hunt little lice on your big, sleek arm . . . they beg you for you know not what, beg you to give them a name, beg you to not let them die without having had a name for at least a moment . . . they weep. . . I saw suffering—which at home is hidden by the sheets and is therefore apparently concentrated in the head—take possession of the monkey's whole body, like hemlock: its feet became cold, then its knees, its hands made the motion of plucking a bird, it sacrificed a parrot to its god of doctors, and then died, she-monkey, the greatest death. . .

It was evident that the traces of a shipwrecked adventurer who had preceded me in this island all belonged to one man; but some of them appeared to date from yesterday while others appeared hundreds of years old. Picks and hooks carried a century of rust; but I thought that I could discern from certain movements of the antelopes that they had formerly been caressed.   One of the monkeys gave the impression that he had been beaten, another that he had been humiliated.   Everything that this man had wished to create in imperishable materials—his house of tree trunks, or his marble shed—I found already eaten with moss or falling into decay . . . but the two dimples, of friendship and of fear, which he had imprinted on two animal hearts, were still visible. He had, too, left his mark on some plants: the parasitic growths respected a bare enclosure at the centre of the island, they respected three old stalks; and the stems of the sunflowers—while their faces obeyed only the sun—were planted according to a scheme which had at first been dictated by a human being.   Not a woman, surely; for he had persisted in lowly tasks that are allotted on desert islands to the strong and energetic sex.   Here, where there is an abundance of fruit and shell-fish he had sown and cultivated rye; here, near two caves which are warm at night and cool during the day, he had cut joists and built a hut; here, where one learns how to climb within two hours, he had constructed ladders, scores of ladders, ranged along the bottom of a valley as though on the eve of an assault or an olive crop; here, where the streams run at varying speeds to quench the most diverse thirsts, he had led bamboo conduits to his hut; here, where the sea was all around, there was a little cement pool, a tub; here, where night equals day, where the sun in unchanging play skips rope with the equator, there were sundials on every flat stone and an old skeleton of a pendulum with bell-springs. . . On the rock that dominated the sea there was cut a metre which was divided into centimetres. . . The Pacific could have measured itself on it to a millimetre. Like a woman who succeeds to a hotel room which has lodged a smoker, I had to air this island, to throw over the stone bench and bamboo chairs some willow screens and feather divans. There, where all is solitude and kindliness, there was carved, in Latin, on the cave: "Mistrust yourself." There were also visible, in a little patch taken from the orchid fields, some miserable flowers: zinias and balsams. . . . Near the tub I found an Italian sou.

A sou doesn't amount to very much, particularly in the eyes of one who has just discovered a treasure; but the fact that it was Italian, that it was the kind of sou which they had refused to accept from me as a child in the cakeshops, a sou which tramps will accept only if they are moving southward, overcame me with astonishment. For I had imagined an Irishman or a Swede alone in an island, but last of all—after

a Belgian or a Luxembourgian—an Italian. . .
Never was my own distress, my own solitude,
clearer than at this moment when I saw an Italian
in my place. The word *solitude,* so supportable in
its Scottish or Danish sense, was discharged at me
suddenly from Italy itself, from its capital. A vision
of all that Italian *solitude* includes—villas, terraces,
fireworks and crowds; rolling of wagons; grape-
vines from which the gatherers, previously invisible,
rise up just as you pass; supreme solitude, under a
bright blue sky, a priest under an aqueduct holding
out his hand to see if the water penetrates and drips;
the solitude of councils; and the Pope, too, almost
alone in his island; and, finally, the great gardens
where one would be alone were it not that when one
is with solitude it is like being with another than oneself—made me comprehend that if I had endured my
island it was just because I had had the strength to
hide all that was Italian in me. I had bribed the terraces of onyx and alabaster with pearl shells so that
they might not haunt me; I had bribed the Pontine
marshes and the Rialto with coral; the cypresses,
pimentos and roses with red fruits big as pumpkins
and with orchids. Latin solitudes that, alas, I discovered thanks to this sou, without having ever
known them; a child that I had never had, yet whose

clothes and playthings I none the less rediscovered!
Portuguese solitude, with vines so thick along the
northern roads that the children make holes in them
in order to see the aeroplanes; and Cintra, where the
vultures, conscious of the altitude, circle ten metres
above men, who always believe themselves at sea
level; where the noise of fountains is deafening at
times when a woman stretches her bare foot toward
the jet of water.   Spanish solitude: with a great
stony soil on which little splashes of silk and velours
—men and women—are strolling; with a vast God-
like silence marked by little points of tenderness and
bitterness,—guitars and mandolins.   In the same
way that one tests a poison on a feebler creature—
absinthe on a lizard, opium on a cat—I poured this
equatorial silence, for a second, into the two wide
Italian eyes held open below me as though to receive
a colyrium. . .   And I saw my Italian woman turn
pale and die!   A Florentine woman alone on a reef,
even near Italy; a Neapolitan woman alone in Sicily;
a Corsican alone, all alone, on the island of Elba:
—what cause for pity!   While on each of the
Tuamotos, the New Hebrides and the Bahamas, a
sweatered English woman springs forth at the
slightest call!

There was nothing else to prove certainly that the

shipwrecked man was an Italian. I went to seek
other proofs, as eager to identify this ancestor as if
he had been my own, as if men reproduced by layering, some generations after their death, without
palpable intermediaries. He was a sailor: one saw
that from the little anchors cut in bark and stone.
He was a man who had left the island and had returned to it: one saw that in animals whose presence
was explained only by trips to other continents.
There were ant-eaters, but not a single ant; and they
ate bark and leaves as they would have eaten ants
themselves. There were mongooses, but not a single
snake; and they revenged themselves on the only
things that snakes have in common with other
species,—on the eggs. I found some bones of animals that had come into the island when they were
already old, or isolated—either the male or the female without the other: a dog, a cat; species thenceforward extinct for me, ancestral species. That was
all. Apart from the ten Italian centimes which I
found in a slot in the coral, as if for this sum the
whole sea would start to play a grand march (the
machine no longer worked; the sea was silent), there
were no other signs except the anchors (distended or
upside down on the bark, intact on the rocks) which
he had thrown out persistently as though in a tem-

pest, and which remained, biting into the mahogany
trees and the amboyanas, without seeing that he had
departed. I vainly tried to find some proof that the
antelope had been caressed; calling him by Italian
names, speaking to him with a Venetian, a Roman,
accent. . . Night had already returned. . . I
raised my arms to yawn, and the monkeys, thinking
that in this way the human maw is filled, threw
fruits down to me from the highest branches. My
domesticated birds from the other island paid me
their last call for the day; the geese and ducks following the current because of the fish, the others
flying straight.

. . . .

I had resolved to swim to the third island despite
its appearance. Seven or eight cable's lengths away,
barren as though she wore a breastplate, she sur-
veyed her two sisters. Not a tree. The wind blew
pollen on to her in spoonfuls, down from the sun-
flowers in quarter-pound lots, and those long-beaked
birds by which mangroves are married, and those
insects, swollen with seeds from strawberry bushes,
which replace layering in Polynesia; but one felt
that she was sterile. She no longer had her ring,
her reefs—a negress near two favorites: illegitimate
wife of the Pacific—and I approached her with a

certain inquitetude. I was already enough at home in the sea to feel that the fish grew less and less numerous with every stroke that I took toward her. I crossed liquid zones which scarcely supported me, which must have been of petrol as when I emerged from the water I found that my tatooings were half effaced. For a whole hour I lounged against a precipitate cliff which must have been of pumice stone as my left side, after having grazed it three times, became as white as it had been in Europe. By a staircase, a real spiral staircase like those which lead down into cellars at home, I ascended, with the sensation of descending, my elbows pressed against my sides, bewaring of little springs that must have been acid. It was from the topmost staircase that I saw the gods. . .

They were lined up by the hundreds, like menhirs; five, ten, fifteen metres high; with enormous heads that contemplated my head which was still on a level with the ground; with noses wrinkled as if they had already smelled me ascending; with cavernous eyes, of which the nearest to me wept little dry tears that were frightened mice. All of them were caught in a silent activity, the glitterings and sparklings of which it seemed to me I had surprised. But I felt reassured at having touched their island only with my big toes. I clambered up the last steps.

I saw them all in front of me, lighted from behind by the sun, with their shadows, in this review, spread out at their feet like soldiers' equipment. All their minds and bodies were on the alert, like Footit's* son when his father asks him if he knows what it is to think. They all questioned themselves in my sight, looking within to see if they knew the answer. All were dusty, like marble commode-tops, offering a superb prey for a kodak, but only the slight movement of their shadows to a movie camera. Out of politeness toward a human being they all tried to receive me by what they believed to be thought: one by a crawling gray bird which moved over him like a louse; another by a frog in his flanged ears which held a purer water than the orchids hold; still another by letting a little worn out arm fall from his giant body. At times I had the impression that they relaxed from their immobility; that a distant one leaned forward, that one near by me stirred. I uttered a loud shout, and was on my guard again.

One quickly learns to distinguish gods. Only one was truly beautiful, only one would have pleased me, with a beautiful part in his hair and a beautiful Adam's apple, like those of the tennis players at Deauville. This one came from an island where

* A popular Paris clown.

they wear collars. There was only one who was truly intelligent, to whom it would have been a pleasure to teach the four seasons, the four operations. He had a lifted nose like a fox. There was a movement in my soul when my glance passed from the one who had a fleeting smile to the one whose smile was eternal. Certain ones appeared false, as though they had been artificially aged by antique dealers. And in the same way that one stands in front of a Louis XVI commode and judges it genuine if one experiences an indefinable Louis XVI feeling, so I placed myself in front of each one of them; I judged him, and experienced an inexpressible Caledonian horror or a Papuan tenderness: they were genuine gods. Certain ones I thought I had seen before. I found them well in the rear, smiling at their trick, having reached their new positions by an oblique or a straight route, like a horse or a fool. The ground around some of them was covered with little idols; this maternity remaining incomprehensible. All were marked with the same design, like a troop of gods which belonged to one man. The cleverest among them, almost guessing what thought was, spoke to me through the voice of a toad hidden in his head; then, spoiled by success, hissed through a snake hidden in his foot. All were embarrassed and humiliated at being convicted of impotence, face to face with this white woman, in the presence of the sea and the breeze that they had terrorized. Two of them so clearly directed their glances toward a corner of the island that I followed their invitation in spite of myself, and, from the last balcony of the terrace I finally saw what it was toward which all were turned: an ocean without an island, the nearest approach to infinity on our little earth. I had to turn around in order to see my two islands once more, lying behind me like two buoys marking the spot where a submarine is submerged. All were motionless as if there were only one real god hidden in their army and it was my task to discover him. And in fact I was seeking him, touching them with my finger, like Ulysses seeking Achilles in the regiment of girls. . . I found him. . . !

So it was that the pendulum of my life, pulled back too far, now swung only from animals to gods. Of a certainty I, like everyone, created the universe. But this machine which had formerly been so perfect—keeping me from late trains, from early calls —could no longer be called accurate. I was no longer capable of anything except those slow movements of the soul which are monkeys and parrots, or those shining figures which are Papuan gods. Soon the gulf would grow broader. At one end of my thought I would have only the animal that is closest to a plant, at the other end God himself. They were my two only neighbors. The least misstep threw me against an armadillo or the Trinity. I was the one person in the world who did not have a million men at his right and a million at his left, with women in between to help deaden the shock, and everything that came from nature or from my heart struck me with its initial force and bowled me over. All those shivers which had come to me through my nurses or my poets, and had scarcely wrenched a sigh from me, now threw me to the ground, now rolled me bloody upon thorns. The horror at knowing Strasbourg to be German, transmitted to me by my tutor, had formerly made me close my eyes at most; now it tore from me, on this sparkling bank, strident cries. The hatred of Lavaliere cravats, which once had made me smile, now made me fling whitish soles against sharp heaps of pearl-shell. My simplest thought did not stop until it had reached its zenith. Try as I might to wink my eyes, to wink my soul, nothing restored me to a world which moved at the Gaumont* pace of mediocre movies, the world in which I would have found my friends again. . .

* French movie company.

At times I felt it would be enough to find a word and to cry it aloud in order to escape from this enchantment. I pronounced at random the first that came to me, trying it on the horizon as on a strong-box; more desirous of a dictionary than of a saviour; certain that if I read it from end to end I must press the right spring: the word which opens Paris, lighted garret-windows; the word which turns on electricity, which lights the gas. . . In vain. . . If a name came into my mind during my siesta, I awoke; I shouted it to the sea. . .

Nothing: a bird.

I told myself that I had uttered it too brutally, that it was necessary to wrap it in two or three in-distinct consonants. I lodged it in this assemblage . . . I hurled it. . .

In the distance there was a very little eddy; but a real little eddy. Then,—nothing more. . . I thought of dying.

But then it was that Calixte Sornin appeared and saved me. His was the first dead man's name that I had ever heard, at my first mass. I knew nothing of Calixte save his name. A peasant no doubt, a laborer. The priest had said that he was a bachelor, an orphan, and ninety-one years old. I was the sole depository of this feeble memory. Once I had

disappeared,—while I had nothing to fear for myself as my memory would live for a sufficiently long
time in Bellac, and in Paris through Simon—once
I was dead the last reflection of Calixte's life would
be annihilated.   At times I felt more responsible
for this memory than for my own existence.   I sustained it with a thousand promises.   I would oblige
Loti to name a book after Calixte.   I would have
a high mass said before the children of Mary and
throw this name into the memories of fifty little
girls, assured that one of them would take it and
nourish it with her life blood.   I would compel the
geographers to call my island Calixte Island, or,
even, to give this name to the island of a thousand
gods, and thus link it in philosophy courses with
the idea of God himself . . .   I was more than a
savant who hesitates to commit suicide because a
discovery will die with him: I had the key, I alone
had the key to a human life.   A human being would
die or live through me.   It would have been cow-
ardice towards him had I permitted myself to go to
the bottom, to hang myself, or to lose hope . . .   So it
was that this name, the first that mourning had thrown
upon me, sustained me above tempests, attaching me
to the ground and holding me in that feeble stratum
of air, two metres high, in which one lives . . .

CHAPTER VII

In the great city of London
He is a creature more alone
Than a shipwrecked man upon an isle,
Than a dead man in his shroud.
Big loafer, little stock-holder.
Jeanne, that's his trade.

Today this strophe returned to me from our little
course in ethics. And this one also:

At Dover a queer fellow
Fell in the canal one day.
He shouted for help.
He clambered on a reef.
But no heart swam toward him. . .
Adèle, thus died the idler.

For our school-mistress, Mademoiselle Savageon,
procured her models of vice and virtue exclusively
from the United Kingdom. Materials, on the contrary, were unhappily ordered from M. Renon of
Boussac . . . So the idlers and the stock-holders

of Europe were more isolated than I! I would have liked to believe it. But at least everyone in Europe had seemed to be happy to me. Perhaps it was because they all smoked; and then I thought of smoking. I tried reeds and dry grass. There must have been tobacco in the island, but I had never seen it, and it was perhaps the one plant that I did not have the wit to burn; for there are few plants and trees —sunflowers or mangroves—of which I now do not know the taste. Tired of smoking—always imitating the happy idlers—I chewed roots, at times discovering the taste of some remedy taken in my childhood. The land of my Raoul medicine (for strengthening the bones) of my Richard powder (for hardening the gums): that was my island exactly. Then I roasted flowers, not dry but blooming, and thence (my mistress had warned me):

> The big Lancastrian Chinaman
> Entices you with flowers
> Then submerges you in odors . . .
> Soon his pipe is your star!
> From the lily to the poppy, Cécile,
> The road, alas, is easy!

and thence came to me the idea of forbidden pleasures. Through a newly cut bamboo I inhaled the

breath of roasting resin and pollen. Then I thought
of cocaine, against which, however, Savageon had
mobilized neither Lord Mayor of Belfast nor the
notary of Bath. No matter if it disfigured me a
bit, if I had to suffer somewhat in the physical good
form which for two years had been the sole object
of my ambition, as though it were by a footrace
that I was one day going to escape from the island.
The berries which I found were spicy and those
which I believed to be poisonous I tried in my nose
and in little wounds opened by fish-bones,—for I
also remembered morphine. Or I would go along
breathing the air, hoping for springs of ether.
Finally I found within myself what I was now
seeking in the tops of trees—dreams . . .

I who never dream felt within myself one morning a new heart, fragile, completely enveloped in a
network of strings, like a Saregueminian stove that
is being moved. I did not open my eyes; the slightest light would reduce it to dust . . . I had
dreamed . . . I had dreamed what would have
scarcely been a dream in Europe: that I got up,
that I breakfasted, that I sewed. The humblest
servant would not have counted that a dream. I
laid the table, I embroidered. I piled up dishes, I
cut bread. These forks, plates and glasses made me

spend the whole day in self-care and in anguish,
affecting me as others are affected by a dream of
Turkestan or of Ceylon. When evening came I lay
down under the same tree, on the same side, hoping,
if not for more active visions, at least for a dream
which would permit me to see and touch again the
objects that had been absent the preceding night:
oil-bottles, egg-cups, and fish spoons . . .

I dreamed of a man.

No radish dish, no knife-rest. A man who was
weeping. No salad plate; no jam jar. A tall, blond
man with large black eyes. No oyster forks. A
man who avowed all to me. He held me in his arms.
He carried me. It was an abduction and an eternal
farewell. We saw each other for the first time,
and we tore to shreds a common eternity. He
hugged me for the first time, and we possessed all
the memories of a long love. No little glass corners
to be slid under plates when asparagus or artichokes
are served; no finger bowls. But a man, hugging
me . . . No silver spoons; no golden centrepiece.
But this fraternal fiancé who spoke to me for the first
time, and not one of whose phrases appeared new to
me. He made the same movement, above stagnant
swamps, to make me bend over and alternately
touch my hair and my foot to the impetuous cur-

rent. He had the same mania for placing each of
his words in a nimbus around his head, of tossing
back and forth with me ivory balls which slipped
from our hands and which we recaptured in anguish.
We went along with the current of the stream, disdaining the furious dogs which had to swim against
it. He had that white horse which I had never
seen before,—the same one . . . I was sobbing . . .
Our only consolation was to pass the balls back and
forth, then to exchange places little by little . . .
How funny he was, with my two little arms hanging
from his shoulders, like one of the gods on the
other island . . . I awakened! . . .

> The Lord Prevost of Edinburgh
> Says that love is a dream.
> But one day he loses his mother . . .
> His tears run constantly.
> Irène, little Irène,
> Love is the great pain.

After that I slept exclusively under the dream giving tree, training the birds to no longer come and
perch there, pressing my left side with my hand,
thinking of the persons I wished to dream about.
This passion lasted for whole weeks. It was not
that my dreams varied; they afforded me hardly
more than one emotion: that pleasure, unknown to

me until then, in which the most contrary feelings commingled, which I called desolation. It was not sadness alone, but distress with every kind of triumph, happiness with every kind of despair, a feeling of unparalleled discovery and irreparable loss; a sob, like a yawn, that won over all the absurd visitors which the night brought to me. It might be Louis XI, raising me with an affectionate gesture, who consecrated me forever to the service of my kings; or it might be my poor sniffling boarding school friends with the hoarse and raucous voice that one has when a sick person has been saved. But my dreams were always laid in Europe, and they differed from European dreams only by reason of the sun shining in them. Even now I am the one person who sees the sun in dreams.

Then came the awakening . . .

I was listening . . . But it was not a poacher's step upon the road. It was not the bellowing of a heifer being led to slaughter, who balks with all four feet—poor uninstructed beast—when he gets as far as the delicatessen shop. It was not the chicken that is trapped in the poultry house to be killed at evening; nor all the rest of the minor murderous occupations which are lighted by dawn in the provinces. Alas! It was all the flowers on

my tree, its own and those of the creepers and catleyas which came forth from its holes, capsized by
the breeze—despair of baobobs—pouring over me
pollen of all colors in such abundance that the dew
with which I was covered was dried as if by a
powder . . .

I waited. Like a wounded man who mechanically puts his hand to his wound I passed my hand
over my body and afterwards lifted it to my eyes
to see what color the dawn had left me today . . .
No more happy desolation: only limitless distress.
Joy swiftly unwrapped itself from hope, like a
snake frightened by his companion on the wand of
Hermes, and disappeared . . . It was not the
clatter of opening shutters or the morning rain on
the cans of milkmaids. It was the paradise birds
emerging from the night like porcelain from an
oven, with a noise sharper than I could have anticipated; and it was myself, kneeling against more
little palm trees, little banana trees and little arau-
carias, and more indifferent to them and to life than
the Belloir clerk in his carriage on the boulevard
Montparnasse when he is bringing his flora back
from an official ball. I stood up, shaking all thought
and all pollen from a body which was sterile for
them, irritated, having left a malleable and generous

world, by the resistance of these trees through which
one could not pass, by these waves which were
liquid instead of being solid, by the eternal, the
ephemeral sun . . . Egoist, I grew thin . . . Jeal-
ous, I no longer ate . . . Self deceiver, I had
neuralgia. It was so serious that I decided to cure
myself . . . One evening, instead of going to lodge
myself under that tree, in that imprint in the moss
which now received me as a silver case does its big
soup spoon, I waited for the night, I lost myself
in it, I breathed it deeply, I bathed my eyes in it,
I did everything with it that one does with eye-
salves and antidotes. To the best of my ability I
chased away all the personages and emotions that
were accustomed to assail me at this hour, swiftly
penetrating my soul and taking possession of it during my sleep. Then, at the greatest known distance
from any tree in the island, I lay down on my back,
my feet together, my hands crossed, and surrendered
myself to a dreamless sleep. . . .

It was a painful state of affairs. Never had my
soul been more played out, more faded; never had
my physical life been more acute. The light around
me was the most vibrant, next to that of ultra-
violet rays; the birds were the most beautiful, next
to invisible birds; the stars were the closest to earth

—that one, just above, the very nearest; the grating of the sea against the coral was the sharpest sound next to that of saws. Between me and the negation of forces there was no longer anything save this last exasperated appearance: even nature's most sombre colors—ochre, black—were at their highest octave. No animals with low voices (I went to the monkey's island only every fifteen or twenty days, having no protection against their attacks); only the super-shrill cries of birds and the metallic noise of their flight. And in addition, for five or ten minutes at evening, the bull frogs,—sole little mouth organs linked with Europe, which, however, uttered as few words as though they were counted for a cablegram. It was at this period, too, that I lost interest in my feather dress, when I renounced all clothing, when it was given to me to see—last contractions of my French life—those movements of my body of which we are ignorant at home, lost as they are beneath dresses and waists. And for myself I did not have even the consideration that a savage accords his own impassibility. My chest and my shoulders were thrown out the instant that I felt frank and loyal. In spite of myself I lifted my head, I stood up at the approach of an animal, with the same dignity which uplifts a first-class citizen of Bellac at the appearance of a second-class person. One day I discovered, also, that I was losing my memory.

I had been unable to resist the temptation to write: and with that knife which I had cherished for two years as my sole weapon and purveyor I had dared to carve phrases on the trees and in the rock. Each eucalyptus at the alley corners bore a street name, sufficiently low to be read at night with one's hands. Then, in the glades, I composed immense words from pieces of coral and pearl-shell, a precarious mosaic which I consolidated with resin and on which I avoided walking. But each step lost at walking was a gain in memory. The island was soon covered with proper names. Certain ones, according to their shells, shone especially at evening. Others, which I had considered most indifferent, suddenly grew purple without reason, and wished to reveal to me some hitherto unknown friendship. I sometimes found birds in them, caught in the glue and battling for their lives against a greedy vowel: king-fishers caught in the word *Hugo,* nightingales in the word *Pape-Carpentier.* They were in confusion the morning after the monsoon. On the beach I placed more solid words, made of garnet rocks which I carried one by one from the

hill, returning to it every moment as a person who
has no fountain-pen does to an ink-well.   Afterward, from the headland, I saw them speak to me
like advertisements . . .   But at each syllable of
this giant writing I felt the same hesitation that one
sometimes experiences in writing a letter.   I needed
to make no participles agree; but the spelling of the
commonest word became bizarre for me.   I wished
to shout them aloud, but never did a pavillion, re-
opened after centuries, give forth portraits and
furniture more worm-eaten than did my memory
after two years of silence.   Table!   Chair!   Bottle!
These modulations seemed strange to me; these
words which were ready to fly away, to escape me,
had an unknown sound.   I called myself: my name
floated around me, no longer dwelling within me,
and I silenced myself in order to escape becoming
some anonymous body.   I called my friends: the
family names appeared, hard and dry like objects,
drawn by bizarre teams which were the first names.
Not merely did the most familiar word come to
me only after an effort, but once I had pronounced
it, it seemed liberated, it became colorless, it im-
pinged no longer on my tympanum.   I was becoming
deaf to Europe.   I resolved to cure myself.   I took
up all words at their very infancy, before they had

been startled and disassociated,—that is to say, at
my infancy. I imagined my first classes. I started
afresh, in order to plant anew in my memory, from
the place where I was born, from the first lessons in
geography or the catechism, from the first phrases
learnt by heart . . .

It was time . . . Of the ten communes in the
canton of Bellac one had already escaped me forever, and the others—Nantiat, Le Breuil-au-Fa,
Blond—were already circling in me like slightly
sleepy insects in a hall whose door is opened: a
little sunlight, and Nantiat and Blond would fly away
forever. One of the capital sins also evaded me,
and hid itself until my deliverance. I repeated the
list of sins twenty times, a hundred times, sometimes at random, sometimes suddenly, in the hope
of surprising myself in the very act of the absent
sin; or trying to discover an indice in my movements
when I abandoned myself once more to what my
friends and I used to call at boarding-school "our
evil self." Stretched out, with my head supported
by a cushion, I watched my body swell with faults
from the air. In vain. Lying, idleness, immodesty,
passed over it like the lightest clouds; envy, gluttony,
and pride arrived on it in an order as inoffensive and
as immutable as that of the prismatic colors. But

the seventh—that capital sin which is, no doubt,
committed ceaselssly in the tenth commune of Bellac
—resisted all the fish-hooks which I placed on my
body and which I thought I stirred by moving my
finger or my tongue. For if I could not rediscover
it through this body, there was no means, no dictionary. I opened my arms, my legs, thumbing it
at hazard. In vain. I looked at my face in the
water, seeking the sin in it, as though searching
in one of those pictures in which children are
supposed to find a fish in a tree or a soldier
between the joints of a window . . . In vain,
I studied myself in the magnifying glass, hoping
that my image would perhaps, come forth
from it a thousand times enlarged . . . I plunged
my hand and my leg into a running stream which
elongated them or made them quite short and round,
submitting them to a torture which only made them
fresher and more supple, washed clean of even pride
and idleness. Or—in the manner that I had rediscovered the word *indigo,* also forgotten, while
looking at a rainbow—I took a European day from
sunrise to sunset, assured that it would be enough
to tilt it and shake it exactly like a prism in order
to have my sin appear in it. But I stumbled on the
memory of a holy day which offered to me—at the

corner of the Rue de Coq, on the promenade, on that
ill-famed place itself—only the three theological virtues and humble citizens with venial sins. Or I persuaded myself that I could come upon it only in the
forgotten commune. I started out once more on all
the walks of my childhood. I followed again all the
tracks that had led me to my goal; through all the
doors of Bellac I repeated my first sorties into the
country, touching with my memory—at twenty steps,
at forty steps from the house—the first tree, the first
grocer's shop that I had ever seen: but both commune and sin held themselves aloof from all neighbouring roads. In consequence—so benignant did
the other creatures in the island seem to me, so little
pride did I feel face to face with gouras, so un-
deceitful face to face with ptemerops, so moderately
luxurious face to face with mother of pearl, and
yet, at the same time, so swollen with unknown
faults and evils—it alone seemed the true sin, and I
felt within myself its terrible presence.

From sins—following in this, moreover, the
sequence imposed by Madame Savageon—I passed
to Academicians. But their ruses are still subtler.
For I shall surprise no one when I say that it was
rare that a movement of my body or a motion of
the stream suddenly indicated one of them to me.

In one day I had barely collected a half-score, despite all that I could do. These I gathered little by little, making them come forth according to their order in the cupola, during the hour which I spent every morning in consolidating my memory; and sometimes, with the monsoon blowing and the river flowing, the name of a new Academician popped into my head from Europe just as a verse comes to an Academician poet. Light arrows, evidently less sharp than those of love; but they touched at least, as much as memory, a kind of friendliness. It was in this manner that Henri de Régnier arrived one noon: I saw a white peacock scratching his tail with his beak, the feathers spread out in two sheafs like the water of a fountain beneath one's finger; and at the mere thought of a jet of water there came to me the Academician who brought with him on the instant a whole world which I had forgotten—jasper, jade, Venetian stucco, and onyx; foreign names, not worn for me, which resisted the termites of my memory better than limestone. In the same way, on the evening of the same day, a half-day behind de Régnier in this race around the world, there came the Academician René Boylesve who was, thanks to a perfect likeness formed by tree branches, for me the most palpable of them all.

Then—this one did not touch me like a dart, but like a stretched elastic that hit me full in the heart—came the Academician Bédier. For his name suddenly brought back to me Tristan and Iseult, whom I had forgotten also. Then two scarlet birds enshrined themselves in my heart: the two cardinals. Then one day, when I saw a gleaming cloud meet a sombre cloud; the Academician Rostand whom I had seen rejoin M. Bonnat. Of all these illustrious masters who, covered with the same title and the same uniform, seem almost identical to the young girls of France, and who are, at least, worshipped with the same passion—a great green and black key-board with sharps that are Barrès and Loti—each one, thanks to the strange influence of Polynesia, appeared to me unique and original. Then, passing through the Academy as through a great trap door, I went from the immortals who are living to the immortals who are dead and was engulfed in a region where—ignorant as I was, alone as I was—I set myself the task of imagining our literature—I was indeed obliged to do it if I wished to really know something of it—of re-creating it.

I tried to guess what was hidden behind all those names of authors and of heroes, of theories and of customs which, even for the oldest school girls, are

hardly more than screens. Those names *Phèdre*
and *Consuelo* which were thrown quickly into our
eyes so that they might dazzle and blind us so soon
as the subject was love; those classic names Racine,
Corneille, Rotrou, which were handed us all in a
lot, like a jumbled bunch of keys, so that we might
not be able to distinguish which drawer in our
hearts each one would open; all these names, once
pronounced, floated around me, refusing to re-enter
my mind by the habitual path. Once the slightest
distiches of Ronsard and Malherbe were declaimed
in this island, they began to prance and gently attacked me like a team of horses whose muzzles have
been dipped in an enchanted fountain. When those
verses of Lamartine and of Vigny returned to me
suddenly on the wind, my one prompter, perfumed
prompter, whose words completely fanned me; when
I saw the stars, so low here, balanced by the breeze
itself, excite a quatrain which was not in them but
which stirred in my memory; when during the night
I awakened suddenly and a verse of Musset or of
Shakespeare came to me, which I repeated almost
astounded and bruised, as one clings to the broken
rung of a ladder; when I amused myself by joining
together all those names which signified nothing to
me but which I felt were full of sense—Syrinx,

Paludes, Théodore, Adolphe—with the care of an ignorant millionaire who collects names for his race horses and his yachts; then I was seized with a maternal languor, unknown seeds grew within me, and one evening I suddenly found myself no longer face to face with tattered sonnets and snips of prose wadded with putty, but with nine persons to whom I had given little thought until now: the nine Muses. In the same way that a child prefers boxes and caskets to their more beautiful contents, I experienced thenceforward my greatest pleasure from the mere names of *genres* and of my new companions. Tragedy, Lyric Poetry, History: not one hid from me. They were as loyal as sins and Limousin cantons are hypocritical, and I turned them loose in the middle of my island: the first time that cassowaries ever encountered Tragedy, or the paradise birds Epic Poetry.

I experienced, too, in plunging myself into the titles of unknown books, all the emotions of a reader whose departures for various books are as different as for trains taken at random. Sertorius, and the Menechmes, and Hamlet, and Aucassin and Nicolette. I imagined their adventures, I clothed them in movements and costumes so clearly defined that since my return to Europe the actual figures have

seemed less real to me. With the aid of old syllogisms and vague remembrances from school I tried
to look behind and comprehend all the habits and
forms of mind and soul whose names we had repeated at boarding school like parrots: Scholastic,
*Marivaudage,** Preciosity . . . And in my heart a
new spring of pleasures opened like a bar. To be
"precious" is to lose hope while hoping forever,
to burn with more fires than one has lighted, to
weave around a revered word a piece of cloth with a
thousand threads. Preciosity is the heart which
darts forth from its darkest hiding place the instant
that it is grazed by a breath or by a thought, kills
it, and sucks its sweet blood. It is Mademoiselle
de Montpensier sucking the sweet blood of the word
love, of the word *lover.* It is Mademoiselle de Ram-
bouillet, covering all cruel words with her white
hand, and thereafter restoring to us the word *Anger,*
the word *Barbaric* robbed of all offense: like detec-
tives who convert a bandit's revolver into a cigar
case which looks like a revolver.

Marivaudage? Marivauder? It is to lie naked,
stretched out on a headland; to look at the sun, to
sigh, and to say: "You do not sigh! You are not

*Affected refinement in ideas and expression. Word formed
on name of author Marivaux.

looking at the sun! You are too hot: undress yourself! . . . " *Marivauder* with Europe? It is to turn one's back upon it; to occupy oneself exclusively in following the antics of a red-bellied green bird upon a baobab, revolving each instant like a signal disk. It is to say: "Europe, you do not exist! You are not full of great stores with show windows, in which kleptomaniacs roam about! How beautiful your cities would be were they built in the country! And romanticism (termed romantism) and alexandrianism (termed hellenism) and catachresis and litotes, and all those names which we held out proudly at examinations to have them punched like subway tickets, I punched daily after my fashion. I had my own alexandrianism, my own romantism, and false litotes more beautiful than your genuine ones. There are, moreover, certain beaten tracks from Homer to Chateaubriand, to which even an ignorant mind has only to confide itself in order to experience accurately—physical impression—the real trend of all human thought. It was only on the road of the present that I could go astray. My creation became confused so soon as it was concerned with a living poet; and I, whom the docile Aeschylus and Shakespeare obeyed, had no control over Jammes or Bergson.

I became particularly exasperated over three
names which were constantly mentioned among
Simon and his friends, three names that were,
moreover, flaming even for the uninitiated, which
were tossed back and forth forcibly or gently, like
the torches of circus jugglers; three names of which
I scarcely knew the spelling, but which seemed to
me, however, fine screw-nuts, slightly loosened—
taking the place of Renan, of Barrès—the only
screws by which we could now fasten our miserable
existence to the world and its mysteries :—Mallarmé,
Claudel, and Rimbaud.   I knew nothing whatever
about them, whether they were living or dead; I
did not know whether the neighbor against whom I
would bump in a station while buying my ticket, or
in a cake-shop while eating éclairs, could never be—
alas!—or might always be—oh happiness!—Mallarmé, Claudel, or Rimbaud.   What joy to see one
of them furious with a coachman, climbing into
a sordid fiacre as into glory!   At times—as when
in a church hung for a funeral service one is disturbed at perceiving the initial of a parent, and is
suddenly fearful for him—a perfume or a breath
indicated one of the three to me, saving the other
two from death.   I no longer thought of anyone
except these three: I named rivers and headlands in

12

their honor.   Or else—shameless hush-money for
God—I persuaded myself that I was responsible for
the three of them; that if I was lazy, if I enjoyed
my insomnia, if I again abandoned myself to cocaine
or to dreams, one of them would die.   In order
to keep them constantly alive I achieved greater
perfection than a vestal; in order to save them from
lost teeth or broken arms I came to take a real care
of myself. If I let my knees grow stiff from lack
of oil, if I did not keep my heels polished up to the
minute, Claudel had been dead for a long time . . .
If I did not separate that quarrelling pheasant and
cockatoo, Mallarmé would die.   I raised my arm
and frightened the combatants: the black cockatoo
flew to a perch, following the pheasant, who twisted
ahead of him like his golden shadow, from branch
to branch.   But Mallarmé's death was at least ele-
vated three metres.   At times it was their families
who were at stake, and once—cruel one—I let
Rimbaud's sister fall from a ladder; and once I
allowed a friend of Mallarmé's to be drowned.

It was during the evening particularly, when I was
falling asleep beneath stars which were so close and
so brilliant that one of them at times seemed to pass
just above my eyelids like a pocket-lamp, that I was
infuriated by these pure spirits.   It was the hour

when I followed the roaring of the billows around
the island and the roar of the monsoon around the
coconut trees, when this spatial solitude bestowed
upon me, even in my own eyes, more nobility than
the solitude of genius can give in Europe. The equal
of these three men, I summoned them. . . . At times
I arose to rearrange the burning sticks on my little
hearth . . . If one of them did not immediately
throw out a blue flame followed by a red flame,
Rimbaud was losing his wife . . . Then, drowsily
turning over the two or three phrases that I had
heard on the subject, I saw Mallarmé give words a
physical power; I saw trees grow at the sound of
his voice, stopping for a moment at the shoots,*
forming a knot of metaphors; I saw a verse of
Mallarmé, like a lotion, give a new flora to garden
corners and to arbors. Then, to each object, to each
tree, to each human being, in short to all those
appearances which are forever impalpable to us,
Claudel—after having thoroughly abused them—
attached, at least, a simile which immediately
was filled, by I know not what law of communicant
vases, with blood, with sap, with resin, and with
the finest liquids . . . A dull noise close beside me,

* Play on words: *rejet* also means carrying over into a
second verse line a word or words that complete the sense
of the first.

followed by a sweet odor, told me that a falling coconut had broken open . . . All the oysters opened
beneath the waters and re-varnished themselves with
pearl . . . A rougette flew from fig to mango
tree . . . Mallarmé did not see it . . . Rimbaud
took the bird by the head, turned it around in his
hands, and at last succeeded in making his companion see it on its return flight from mango to
fig tree . . . Love? In the presence of this sky
which for three years had been heaped with my
dearest stars, unencumbered by the two chariots,
why did I suddenly think that they might have
spoken of Love? And suddenly I became indifferent to everything that Racine or Musset had said
on the subject, feeling that I must wire my humble
head-bulb to these three new systems. . . . I shook
it in the night, adjusting it little by little to the first
wire that came to me from the shadows; and all of
a sudden I was struck by so sharp a thought, by
so strange a blow, that I guessed they too had felt
it; and when I awoke I found my hands quite black
because of the embers; but I was also like a servant
who is convicted by this trick of having touched his
master's strong box.

It was, however, thanks to these exercises and
these factitious joys, thanks to these shadows and

these surnames, that one fine day (in the same way
that a man, who is learning the language of a foreign
country in which he is living, awakes after six
months of complete deafness and understands everything that is said by the maid in the morning,
then all that is said by the car conductor, then everything said by the great tragedienne in the evening) I seemed suddenly to understand my brother
men.

A seam yielded in the round, impermeable form
with which I had unconsciously enveloped them, as
one puts little bags over grapes on the vine. I had
the same revelation of men that others have of God,
who was, too, very close to me. All the judgments,
which I had learned to apply mechanically to their
vices and their virtues, appeared suddenly inapplica-
ble. Stupid grafts, prejudices, common sense, and
good taste fell away from me outworn, shriveled
by this tropical sun. The sun rose; I saw it rise for
the thousandth time, but, nevertheless, it was as
though I had raised the wick of a lamp for the first
time. Such a light flooded the world that everything which, until now, I had called crime or fault
or turpitude was washed in it. Perhaps I understood light for the first time on this day. Theft;
murder? I saw the adorable moon above the thief;

I saw the setting sun caress the bare arms of the criminal. I saw a tender ray of light accompany the adulterous bodies. I saw the light of an electric lamp shining on the shriveled face of the mother whose son has flunked his examinations. I saw the light from a Venetian lantern illumine the forehead of an unforgiving father,—and he was forgiven. Beneath their lamps I saw the splendid craniums of savants, on which the pessimist's hatchet is blunted as on an oak knot. I saw a bare arm,—was it lighted from within?—moving in the night; a hip lighted by a fire of vine-shoots; and—oh light which travels twenty thousand leagues an hour!—after ten years, after fifteen years, not reaching me until today, the true glances of my friends came to me at last.

It was day-break. From the midst of bell-flowers, whence fell a vivid red pollen, the birds shook not their feathers but their very color . . . I understood crinolines, leg-of-mutton sleeves . . . I understood all those great movements of the earth on which Copernicus and Newton are carried along with the generality of mankind, like the proprietors of tread-mills and moving sidewalks at fairs. Dear little humanity: without this awakening it would for me have always passed fraudulently upon its star; but this morning it was pierced by a single ray of light, as a thief hidden in an Innovation trunk is pierced by the needle of a customs officer. . . . Did it not, moreover, cry a little? Didn't I hear the cry of a child or a lover? An inexplicable internal sweetness, a languor seized me; the odor of the flowers became too strong and made me faint . . . Humanity installed itself within me like a son . . . My two domesticated paradise birds—which I wished were alike and which never were because they were tamed only by couples—bent down on each of my shoulders, and I capsized on the side of the heaviest . . . Ah! How well I understood that fool in Limoges who added to everyone of his phrases, whatever its import, the three words "like a man" or "like a woman." How delightful to imitate him! I reveled in this hour as though it were the first hour of the world; the first hour when, over there, three hundred million men were sleeping, three hundred million were eating, with some scores of millions consecrated to embraces. This morning was my creation . . . I was overwhelmed with love for those fine gangs of workmen. I loved everything that had formerly shocked me. I loved red beards, warts, and eye-glasses. I loved drunkards and merchants, I understood those antique shops at the exit of the Montmartre cemetery, in which I had formerly detested seeing heirs dispense the first thousand francs of their legacies. I understood all those Saturday marriages at Saint-Sulpice, all at eleven sharp in the twenty-two chapels; the grooms with a day-old hair-cut and shaven necks seated on twenty-two stools as though for electrocution. All those masculine glances which had formerly fitted in my eyes as awkwardly as a key in the wrong lock now entered them like a watch-key and wound up all the weights of my heart . . . The jacanas uttered a thousand inhuman cries, like a man. The Kuro Siwo lifted the horizon lightly like a swollen vein, like a woman . . . How sorry I felt for them! How much trouble they mistakenly created for themselves with tramway conductors Russian loans, and negroes! I wished them happiness, eternity. I wished them the alcohol that sobers, the soot that whitens . . . So strongly did I feel that when the sun came forth from his bull-pen astounded, and harassed by two great clouds, it was those people over there, in their billions, who seemed to me suddenly isolated and lost . . . And all day long my solitude had in it a certain poignancy, anguish, and sweetness,—which did not seem to belong to solitude, but to love.

What have you seen in your exile?
Said Spencer to his wife,
At Rome, Vienna, Pergama,
And Calcutta? Nothing! . . . he said . . .
If you wish to discover the world
Close your eyes, Rosemonde.

CHAPTER VIII

O N one of those rare days that I did not permit
to flow anonymously away like thousands of
others, but which I rebaptized by their European
names insofar as they brought me the taste or habits
of a particular day; on the third or fourth day that
I desired to drink intoxicating wine, to eat éclairs,
to dance the polka; in short, on a Saturday I thought
that I saw a movement out to sea. At the extreme
edge of the horizon a shape had run from one wave
and had dived into the next, as a rat in Paris runs
from the railing of one tree to a neighbouring railing. If we had not been taught in school (and
made to copy the fact twenty times, along with the
distance of the earth and the moon, as the most
useless thing to little Bellac girls) that one always
sees the sails or the masts of a ship before seeing
its hull, I would have sworn that I had seen a ship.
If we had not also heard it repeated that hope
spreads the clavicles and dilates the vasomotors, I
would have sworn—with shoulders suddenly sunken

and arteries suddenly compressed—that I had just
been traversed by hope. I turned around toward the
island, looking at it as one looks at the face of a
friend in a forest when one hears steps; but the
island had never appeared calmer. Barring an un-
believable hypocrisy in the island, I was mistaken.
All those gears and gauges of which I will tell you
presently indicated serenity: the spangle on rock
Rimbaud glittered; the little leaf was motionless.
I calmed myself: I went down to take my evening
bath.   Suddenly I was compelled to regain the
lagoon, to touch land as quickly as possible, to run
up on the beach as if the sea had suddenly become
a danger.   In the distance two cannon shots had
sounded. . . .

I had never heard a cannon, but that was certainly
what it was. Besides, only I, the European, had
been affected by this discharge. Nothing stirred in
the island. It was now completely night. The birds
with their heads under their wings had heard nothing. So there were men over there! I did not
want to wait for daylight; I wanted to swim toward
them immediately, surrendering myself to the Kuro
Siwo as one takes a local train in preference to
waiting for an express. Was it a signal? Had a
whole ship fired to ask counsel of me? Was I the

sole recourse of a hundred sailors, of a hundred
people in distress . . . Suddenly I saw two flashes;
and I waited, counting with greater agony than if
I were awaiting two shells:—and the sound of the
two shots came to me!

Then four; then six; then a silence. Then twenty,
thirty; the flashes of two new shots exactly coincided
with the sounds of the two preceding: I heard and
saw them simultaneously. Then fifty, then a hundred: they were scratching a whole box of matches
on the sky. Then a lone shot, whose flash I had not
seen although my eyes had never left the horizon.
The whole island was now awakened. It was bright
moonlight; all the birds were flying about, the day
birds, in long bands, striking against the stupefied
night birds. Their colors which I always saw sep-
arately and at the same altitude, were commingled
and unbalanced: the aquatic birds soared in the sky,
the humming-birds alighted, and for the first time
the orange crow came down to my level. Never
was a kaleidoscope more thoroughly shaken than
my island was that night: not one of the combina-
tions was forgotten. A rocket rose, first cleaving
the stars, then cleaving the night. The last time that
I had seen a rocket had been that night on the roof
with Ceorelle, July 14th. Perhaps it was another

celebration. Or was a king's son born? Or twins? For they had fired more than a hundred at once . . . Suddenly the rays of a searchlight walked on the waves, (how slowly!) halting stupidly over little eddies with which I was familiar and which I knew were hardly a metre deep, turning and returning around a bit of foam like a horse around a hat: at last it reached the island. It remained puzzled for a moment, perplexed at having struck a solid mass. I ran toward it, brushing by the birds which fled from it, stretching my hand toward it like a drowning man reaching for a rope. It moved on a few metres. I once more won the center of the shaft, and stood directly in the path of its middle ray; I waved my arms, I writhed, I shouted. But, like the glance of a friend which touches you in a crowd without recognizing you, which sees you wave your arms, writhing and naked without recognizing you, it suddenly lifted, straightening up like the smokestack of a ship which has passed under a bridge, rising to its full height under this obscure arch, and went out.

I had tried in vain with my magnifying glass to set fire to a piece of bark from this light. To make a fire I had to wait for the sun. . . . Suddenly a last cannon shot reverberated, farther off but sharper.

A kind of revolver shot to finish off a dead beast or a man. It was the first that I understood. The first that announced to me that kings had no sons, captains no birth-days, France no July 14th . . . that there was war!

.   .   .   .

My fire was lighted by the sun's first ray, the purest, the coldest ray; I had prepared my funeral-pyre of dry leaves, of tinder, and of cork. It flamed up. For the first time I let the fire bite into the neighbouring shrubs and grasses . . . I was ready to burn my island as others have burned their vessels . . . But of the night's terrible secret nothing was apparent in daylight. The birds' paths, untangled from the skein of yesterday, were once more straight and brilliant threads. An ignorant sun was shining. The ptemerops, the adjutants had forgotten everything. The trouble which had departed at morning was no longer shared by me with the island and its inhabitants, and I felt in my heart even a new solitude in my loneliness . . . So war had grazed the island with its glance and had disappeared on its drifting ship, without my having to menace it with a pole and a boat-hook as I had been compelled to do in the case of the couguar on his raft! . . . And what war? What maritime nations

had dived into the sea to come up here and fight
before a single witness, seeking to destroy their great
gills by cannon shots? In what language were they
now saying: "My son is dead. My father is dead."?
In what language were they saying: "They are
coming" or "At last they are leaving"? In what
language was a stuttering envoy announcing the . . .
the . . . announcing that the army was . . . was,
in short, tapping with his foot, announcing war? A
thousand leagues away from it, I felt myself restored, like all women, to a mass from which men
have the right to choose. What races of horses and
of mules would die from suffering and cruelty?
What lake cities would smell ether and iodine? In
what stations would Duchesses hire a statistician so
that he might direct the seriously wounded to their
proper branch-lines? I paraded war over a map of
the world, trying it on each country, like the cover
of a long or oval box; and, with a little forcing, it
fitted almost all of them. In what language were
they saying: "Finish me!" I hesitated to choose, as
if by this choice I would give the signal: I hesitated
between Germany, and Austria, Spain and the United
States. War, which suddenly detached the heraldic
animals from the blazons of great empires and made
them battle silently to the death for me: the unicorn

against the bear, the single-headed eagle against his colleague with three heads! Then I thought egotistically—least anxiety, worst tenderness—that perhaps only two small nations were at war: Cuba, for example, with Bolivia; Peru with its northern neighbour with the Equator for the front. Or, if it was necessary to bring a European people in at any cost, perhaps it was only Norway against Panama, Denmark against Uruguay. . . . I pronounced the names of all the capitals aloud, seeking in the air a secret padlock which stirred at times,—impassible at the word Paris. . . . Yes, it was certainly by the word Copenhagen, the word Lima, that I opened within myself a well of pity: poor Danes, hoisting their cannon for a last stand to the top of their highest mountain, fifty-three metres high! Poor thousand Limeneans, when in the streets of Lima the trumpet sounds announcing the list of dead, all closing their immense eyes at the same second! . . . It calmed me a little to confide this war to such innocent hands. . . . War, which suddenly turns entire hostile nations a single color, that they scatter in the fields to exterminate it: Germany, madder-red; Russia, Turkish green; Italy, white. . . . All those cuirassiers' horses that come back, each one eating the tail of the horse ahead, until there is not one tail

in the whole squadron save on the helmets! All
those millions of men going away, choosing ascep-
tic and well sharpened weapons, each one bolstering
up his own courage as if each one had to kill himself. . . . An American war, no doubt; but nevertheless I did not succeed in calming Europe within
me. Certainly I saw France at peace, yet I already
felt my sentiments toward other countries, toward
all of them, vacillating, vacillating: I felt some unknown poison overcome the love that I had felt for
Spaniards, my confidence in the English, my friendship for Bavaria; and Madrid, London and Munich,
round on their plateaux, were now no more than the
sections of a roulette wheel, grazed ceaselessly by
a ball which touched now at Lisbon, now at Tokyo.
Oh! I hated that sound of cannon, stilled perhaps
forever, like the voice of a woman who reveals to
her husband at the instant of her death that one of
his friends has betrayed him, dying just before con-
fessing the name, and eternally spoiling for him
both great and little friendship.

.   .   .   .

I was accustomed to go to rock Claudel at noon.
The current grazed the island just at that point,
everything sent me by the universe landed there,
and I visited it as the sole distributing station of the

13

postal service which had formerly brought myself.
Every month a cast-off thing from Europe or an
almost new present from Oceania awaited me there,
but most often I returned at the end of one or two
hours with nothing but my shadow. On this particular day, held against the rock by the current,
pressed against it by an insistent sea, there was floating the body of a dog. It was already swollen. It
was indeed the very animal whose cadaver is the only
corpse that one sees often in France, which renders
the worst destiny familiar to French children. But
here, thanks to the eddy, it maddened itself in an
effort to get out of the water, to draw this symbol
of death to dry land. I pushed it away with as many
blows of the boat-hook as an English policeman who
sees a real live dog landing in England. It was a
poodle. It drew off for an instant and then returned, in a movement of the sea which, without
knowing it, replaced the reflex action of a beaten
poodle. It was drifting away at last when I spied its
collar. I swam toward it, undid the buckle, and it
went off, its mission terminated having brought me
these two incomprehensible words: Volga, Vermeer.
Some minutes later a heavier mass passed by in
the offing; another dog, a Newfoundland, which
also gave me two words: Kismet, Bellerophon.

Poodles, Newfoundlands,—faithful races, which came to seek me out even here, and which would surely have brought the shepherd dog with them had he not been held in the middle of the Brie by duty.

Suddenly there sounded the call by which my birds announced that a new bird had penetrated the island. But instead of pursuing the intruder from cocoanut tree to baobab, in long red or green lines terminated by the slowest black cockatoos, they crowded around some piece of wreckage by the edge of the sea. They hid it, but they outlined a shape around it. I saw under all these wings a giant statue, an upholstered figure; swollen and palpitating. As I approached I too was surrounded and covered with a veil of excited birds, I too became a giant aerial creature with a woman's small body at the centre. I arrived. The first among my parrots were already mingling with the parrots around the wreckage. I leaned over, thrusting aside the birds which covered it like a blanket. I saw a shoulder, and it was immediately hidden by new feathers. For a moment I fought against this envelope which split in places and allowed me to see a knee, then a hand, then a smooth surface as though there were a human soil beneath. Then I must have touched the hook-bird of this dress for they all flew away at once and, the clothing vanished; I saw a man.

A man who came to me naked, as a child comes to European women. The upper part of his body lay dry upon the sand, but the water rose to his waist; modest as he was in death. His arms were outstretched; he seemed crucified on my island as though Oceania wished to make an example of him. When I first glanced at the body of this man, the first I had even seen, I was stupefied at being able to decipher his life and his slighest habits! Had I, then, so much knowledge of men? The index finger of his right hand was yellow, which meant that he was a smoker; his heels were worn and run over like shoe-heels, which meant that he was authoritative; the mouth, opened sideways, indicated that he had amused himself by long-distance spitting; the pushed forward upper lip told me that he was gay, that he loved puns; his waist which was corrugated and wrinkled by a belt proved him a gymnast. He had close clipped red hair and a new beard; the crew had been shaved and clipped in anticipation of the battle. His nose was broken: later I thought that he must have been a boxer. On one side, from his knee to his shoulder, was a line of scars like notches as though a child had been measured against him every year. His lips were closed exactly like

those of a man who has just spoken; but his face
was hard as though awaiting no response : a pleasan-
try, no doubt, regarding the torpedo that was coming
toward them.   Certain other indefinable signs, distributed over chest and hands, indicated trickery and
lies.   But I hardly considered the imprudence of
giving myself a master who was tricky and
lying, a master who spit, and already I was bent
down over him.   I could not pull out his tongue for
it was impossible to open his jaws, nor could I sus-
pend him by the feet for he was too heavy, nor work
his arms back and forth as they were already too
stiff.   For an hour I circled around him, beseiging
his body in order to give him life, with as much care
as one uses to kill a turtle or any other shelled animal,
seeking a chink in his armor, trying to burn him
with my magnifying glass, as enemies formerly did
in real sieges.   In vain.   Stretched out in the form
of a cross on the coral to which I had dragged him,
he at once restored to me only the standard of my
religion and my race.   At times, seated at his bedside
I watched over him like a typhus patient.   He restored to me the old Occidental measures by which
to judge this world in which I had become the only
norm : the inch, the cubit, and the ell.   Sometimes I
caressed his forehead as though he were feverish.

As the sun rose, the shadows on his face constantly modified his features without, however, his ever resembling anyone I knew; exhausting the faces of a series of human beings whom I had never met. He was covered with tattooings which were at first indistinct on his bluish body; but the sun revealed them little by little like a sympathetic ink, and I read them as fast as they appeared on him. First of all, his first and last name: this was English; this was the body of John Smith. Then his nickname: for the ladies this was Johnny's body. Then a taunt for the one who would read his tattooings; but I did not get angry at him. Then a phrase from the Bible dedicating this body to Him who made the mountains skip and who calmed hearts: this was Johnny Smith's soul. On his left arm, beside three little anchors in a triangle and the marks of vaccine which liberate one forever from earthly ills, were two words in old characters of the seventeenth or eighteenth century: ROYAL NAVY. Then, where tattooers insist on believing the heart is located—exactly in the middle of the stomach—was a life-sized heart with an arrow. Scattered feminine names: Mary, Nelly, Molly, with dates and towns. Mary of Plymouth, Nelly of São-Paulo, Molly of Dakar. Johnny was faithful to English girls in all

continents. On one of his legs the tibia and femur
were outlined, one foot showed all the little bones;
and on the sole was the signature of the artist:
MACDONALD, TATTOOER TO THE KING,
JERMYN STREET. On the chest in letters five
centimetres high was the beginning of a phrase, I
AM, which I succeeded in reading in its entirety
by turning the heaviest page that I have ever read
in this world below: I AM A SON OF HAPPY
LEEDS. A son of happy Leeds, of rich Leeds,
more alive with hat-pins and hair-pins than a divan.
Despite myself I was reading aloud, with interrup-
tions to chase away the birds, in the language of
Johnny Smith. With him I spoke nothing but
English. Kneeling before him, I saw England more
clearly than if a thousand vessels flying the Union
Jack had passed in the offing. . . . So, according to
the law of averages and probabilities, it was an Englishman that the sea brought me! Of all bodies floating on the waters, the number of Englishmen
surpassed by one at least that of the sailors from all
the rest of the world put together. The two-thirds
law applied to English sailors and English poodles
as well as to battleships. At the first sound of cannon which rent my waves to their depths, John
Smith came to me, like a Gaul's skull from under

a plow in Berry; a swollen body, a sponge that had
been passed over England, musty with gin; a blotter
pressed over those words *Nelly* and *Molly;* one of
those English bodies whose density is less than that
of sea water; a calming oil which is spread about
boats in a tempest; an Englishman dead by drowning. . . .   But the idea of John Smith dead by
drowning, instead of troubling me, gave me almost
as much calm and confidence in destiny as the idea
of a Florentine dead by stabbing, or a Swiss dead
at the age of a hundred years.

Night was falling: the most excited birds, overcome by sleep, were flying away from our group,
going to put under their wing the beak that had
pecked a human being; and before long I was alone
with him.   I could not make up my mind to drag
him to one of the coral bathtubs that I fixed on as
his tomb.   The moon rose, passed over him and
silvered him like a toilet article.   Excepting my
grandfather he was the first man I had ever sat up
with in my life: for this stranger from Leeds I had,
at each instant, only a filial gesture.   As in the case
of my grandfather I could not bear being at his
side; I felt myself useful and confident only when
standing at his feet, at the very axis of his life;
forming above Death—formerly with the dying

man, this evening with the drowned man—very
nearly the same group as the man and his wheel-
barrow above Niagara. I dared to lean only in his
direction, because of vertigo. Each slightly noisy
wave, each gliding creeper, each falling cocoanut
made me shiver as if he were linked by invisible
threads to the fruit, to the branches, to the birds—
an Englishman, to each wave—and as if every noise
was evidence of a secret movement within him. I
contemplated him. I now had almost complete
knowledge of his body, and I could discover only
two little imperceptible traces of his shipwreck and
his death: one closed eye more swollen than the
other—this one had, doubtless touched the water
first—and a scratch near the shoulder. Fresh
wounds which I tended like those of a living man!

When I had learned all about him; when I had
exhausted him like a newspaper; when I had circled
around him, close by and at a distance, as never an
Englishwoman turned around a statue in a museum;
when my whole island had been rebuilt like a European city, and my thought also, from the ladder of
a man, then I threw over him armfuls of night-
blooming flowers,—his last clothing, more vibrant
and adjustable than the garment of birds, and
noisy before long, for all the big night bees came

to buzz in it. Occasionally I fell asleep for an instant: from an aeroplane anyone would have thought he saw a sleeping couple on the island. I amused myself by this game for an invisible spectator: I lay down near the body, I seated myself beside it, I fell asleep above its outstretched arm. I awoke, and at a leap I again took possession of this dead man in my thought, as ardently as one seizes the hand of a big sister at night in France. I waited for daybreak. Since it was no longer possible to save him from the shades, I wished to save him from this last night. Suddenly the sun arrived; the little birds, now less curious, busied themselves with their meal, and the body was now outlined only by the immense wing-spread of some vultures, lost in the sky, that I had never seen before. I immediately felt that sharks were on the road from some distant depth, swimming toward us at the speed of light. I knew that flies, called from another archipelago, were flying in a straight line and would soon arrive. I sensed the clamor of all that Pacific agency which superintends burials of so high a class. I felt the departure, at twenty thousand leagues an hour, of the light rays that were going to show him to me, more livid, more emaciated, green and unworthy. I made up my mind then: I dragged him as far as the red bathtub, slipping round pieces of wood under his body so that I could roll it; and he left on the beach—but with an opposite meaning—the imprint of a jolly-boat that has been launched. Never had my footprints been so distinct as under the weight of this man, and I experienced the same anguish when I turned and saw my deep tracks that I would have felt at the sight of a stranger's.

I was hungry. I was hungry with a new hunger. After the first work that I had done in the island— or, perhaps, simply from contact with this English carnivore—I longed for more than oranges and bananas. I was hopeless; but I had a sudden appetite—recompense of labor; consolation of burials— for pickles, roast beef, chicken en casserole . . . My birds circled around me without suspecting the change . . . I wanted to go fishing and broil trout over charcoal. Suddenly, as I was throwing into the sea a round fruit which had struck me; as I was vainly trying to chase away a bee; as I was thinking sadly that I was there—repeating exactly the movements of Nausicaa* and Sakuntala†—and that only a

* The daughter of Alcinous, King of Phœnecia. See Homer's *Odyssey*, lib. VI. She rescued Odysseus when he was cast up on the coast of Phœnecia.

† A water-nymph in Hindu mythology; but best known as a character in the famous Sanscrit drama Kélidása.

single shadow spied me; as I was feeling within myself more tenderness and devotion than was ever required to make a heroine, more of the art of swimming, of climbing, of hitting any cocoanut with a stone; and feeling that all these things were unfruitful, then—as if looking fixedly at death made you see it thereafter a hundred times—suddenly (I had the same terror as a philosopher who feels that his thought is not following links and locks, but is teemingly reproducing itself like a culture) I saw corpses approaching from every direction. They were landing where living men would have landed: a score of them were spread out for this assault. From all the little creeks by which I emerged from my bath a man was now emerging. Others, caught in the current, passed by in the offing; each with his own swimming stroke (champion in death of the over-arm); shoulders out of water, and arms sticking up; there a head, there a hand, there a foot: by scraping the surface of the sea I would have had the wherewithal to reconstruct Johnny's whole body. But for the most part they were stuck against the bank, tirelessly wearing themselves out against the pumice stone and pearl shell with those infantile jerks that the thrusts of the sea give to us.

.   .   .   .

How dissimilar men are,—so light, so heavy, so fine, so coarse, so vulgar, so worthy even in death that I could distinguish the appreciative from the ingrates among these cadavers! After each rescue I rested, but not before I was almost modeled by a half-hour's contact or embrace with a man of a certain form; and I was disoriented for a few moments in the presence of the succeeding body—a clothed body when the other had been naked; supple when the other had been stiff—forcing my arms and my piety to espouse twenty different forms. At times the moon lighted the drowned man and I became accustomed to his face; at other times I fished up a body in the shadow, and later, on the bank, I could not recognize it; it seemed to have arrived without my aid. Sometimes an unexpected wave pushed the body; I felt that it was helping itself . . . The sun returned. The sea had changed color at each body drawn from it: purple at the one before the last; and, suddenly empty of death, completely blue. It was, however, the first day in years that I did not bathe . . .

I counted them: first I found seventeen, then sixteen; then the missing one reappeared. Some had their heads, others had their feet turned toward the sea. Around each head some bird was always flying; so much more curious are birds regarding faces than bodies. One had a little bell in his pocket, and it rang. Two wore wedding rings: thereafter I had two wedding rings on the same finger. The youngest one, beardless, was wearing a black jacket with gold buttons like those worn by our school boys: nothing was missing, neither cravat, nor watch, which a schoolboy has on his return from vacation. The clothes were made to measure, the kind that the sea does not succeed in removing from the body; the belt was fastened to the cloth by clasps and the midshipman held his hat in his hand,—the one object that he could have lost in the disaster. The mild fear of losing his cap, mingled with a confidence in his collar and in his boots, illumined and sanctified this face. But as the sun warmed it, I saw this company, which I had thought was uniform, divide in two. The alliance that all the drowned men had formed against the night was broken. There were two kinds of sweaters, two kinds of caps; which meant that there had been two ships. There were two kinds of heads and hands, two positions even in death; there were two styles of hair cutting, which meant that there were two races . . . Then I saw war.

First: the company of seven white-skinned giants,

all young and all of equal height like a mythical
people; most disfigured and most swollen, as though
they were not accustomed to death in the ocean; their
faces so fat and their mustaches so pomaded that
the water rested on them in little drops without
having disarranged a hair; one of them with a mus-
tache-holder, all with instruments, in their pockets,
which are quite useless at the bottom of the sea—
harmonicas, little flutes; all with their names marked
on their sweaters in indelible ink, but innocent of
tattooings and anonymous as soon as they were
naked; their finger-nails polished; and each face
bearing a resemblance, not to some stranger
glimpsed in an orchestra or a coach as is the custom of dead men, but an exact resemblance to the
comrade at his side.   And then: ten sun-burned
muscular bodies, with necks like seals', with brass
wire for hair, with horns for nails, and gold for
teeth; all different and all resembling (had I then
forgotten what men resemble?) dogs, horses and
house-dogs; one looked like a cat, the midshipman
like a woman; all with pockets empty save for tobacco and pipes; but almost every body carrying its
name and address—one with the same Nelly of
Dakar, another with the whole battle of Hastings,
and a third whose life was described from his neck

down in five or six lines (birth, engagement, shipwreck of the *Sunbeam,* shipwreck of the *Lady Gray*)
while there remained, for the inscription of his death,
the whole sternum which had doubtless been
jealously reserved for women's names; and, last of
all, there was one who bore upon his arm (this
alone urged me to take sides between the two
races) : *Souvenir de Boulogne et un pavillon français.* It was seven German sailors against ten of
Great Britain; it was—thanks to their names I
could identify these rivals—Meyer against Blakely,
Waldkröte against Parrott. It was those open
mouths, those rolled back eyes, those land dwellers
who rode upon the sea thanks to some trick, without their density being of any aid, with fingers so
fat and wide-spread that it might have been said
they had no palms, against ten bodies with clenched
teeth and closed eyes, so emaciated that it seemed
as though the sea instead of swelling them like the
others had sucked them, and taken back a heritage
from each Englishman. That was what they were
doing over there without me! It was England
against Germany . . . I was suddenly astonished
at not having been forewarned by a more formidable
noise . . . I gave ear . . .

The sea was once more king's blue, colored by

that last dead man that no one will ever see withdrawn. The wind drove toward me a wave which
now seemed empty, although insistent,—a wave
without a human being. The ocean made me all
those signs by which a dog tries to tell that his
master is dead or dying near at hand: advancing a
step toward a stranger, licking his feet, taking a
step backward, turning off in a useless direction.
The night flowers on Smith were withered. The
birds were pilfering young worms along the
shore, and from each falling cocoanut, as from a
shell, as soon as it touched the ground, there came
forth darting flames that were the birds of paradise.
The sun, in accordance with the slant of the cadavers, was already touching some of the faces and
pointing them out to me. I would have to hurry,
for all those beasts that I had never seen in the
island—multipeds and necrophores—coming by a
subterranean route from their last bird's corpse to
their first man's corpse, were already rising up
around each body, and around each one too, in order
to delay this last departure, were the birds crunch-
ing insects . . . I did not have time to dig so
many graves. I decided to throw all the bodies into
the largest coral pit, and I commenced with the
Germans nearest it. It was they who enriched me,

laden as they were with rings, bracelets and golden chains. Their belts, wallets and pockets were of india-rubber that the water had been unable to penetrate, and all of them had become impervious to the sea under the same imperial law which, on the contrary imposes on them pervious faces and hearts, sensible to wines and to chateaux, when they penetrate France greedy for her seasons. Already I felt in effect that France herself was also menaced in this war. From each body I sought a sign that would tell me which of these crews had died for me: I hoped to divine it by standing up suddenly, by embracing them with a glance . . . Still nothing. Not a sign. And I stooped down for my harvest of fish-scales, precious stones, seaweed, and insects preserved in herbariums: all that this seven-toothed rake had raked up from the Pacific. It was not until I came to the pocket of the last German that I found the *Petit Éclaireur de Shanghai;* and a headline in immense type informed me that in Champagne—I learned of our victories first, which helped me bear the news—one of our patrols had taken a prisoner . . .

I was alone with my allies . . .

Sometimes, when I was tired of dragging too heavy a body, in the same way that one turns from

a knotted lace to untie the other shoe first, I let it
go for one that was more supple. . .

.   .   .   .

I did not wake until the next day when the sun
was already sinking. It was the only day in the
island of which I had seen only half and which
I could subtract from the total of the others. I was
stupefied with sleep. I let myself speak out loud
according to habit, knowing that my most mechanical words informed me regarding myself.

"Suzanne," she said, "you are alone . . . "

And in truth my solitude had been wound up
again like a clock. I rose. Of those who had
troubled the island there remained only some light
tracks that looked like the marks of aeroplanes
which have landed. I rambled along the shore: once
more I put myself at the service of this war which
counted on me to touch the extreme point of its
rays and to free it from the dead man which each
ray wore like a hat . . . But why, after all, be
sadder than day before yesterday? I had gourds
full of rum; I had fountain-pens and ink: I could
get drunk; I could write a letter. I had everything
that linked seven German sailors to the world and
made them prefer life to death. I had one of

those ten pfennig pieces for which one can circle
Heidelberg in a red tramway or Munich in a blue
tramway; one of those half-marks which are suffi-
cient to make the chief guardian in the Berlin museum turn Rodin's *Eve* around on its rolling pedestal
for you, while the poor can see *Eve* only from
the front or have to walk around her; I had one of
those *louis d'or* for which one can go from Coblenz
to Bingen on an old ship that has Bettina Brentano
drawn in silhouette on the deck where she slept
while going to see Goethe. I had twelve post-cards
showing views of Singapore, and a picture of the
octopus, the very one, to which Toulet threw the
lobsters . . . I had five harmonicas, and two flutes:
I tried them . . . I had the whistle to which the
poodle must have answered . . . I had the tinder-
box of the man who looked like a Frenchman,
whom I had buried the one before the last; the
cashmere handkerchief of the midshipman whom
I had buried last, so that his parents might be
satisfied, so that he might be the last to leave his
last deck; the notched knife of the Irishman whom
I had drawn from his wave by the feet, the heaviest,
and who seemed all day, at two paces from the
water's edge, like a seal who had been felled at the
moment he was regaining the sea. I had learned

all that one woman, in repulsion and in pity, can learn from men; I had everything that twenty contesting men could throw as pledges into the apron of a young girl: carved rings from Rotterdam, spectacles, bunches of keys with which to open, first, twenty chests and cases at the bottom of the sea, second, twenty cupboards in Wiesbaden or Cardiff, plus a big key like a cellar key. I had a picture of Sophie Silz in evening dress, posed in front of the canvas sea that photographers arrange for sailors' sweethearts; Bertha Krappenau, in man's clothes, dressed like a Tyrolean, but beside a real lake on a real stile; and I had the *Petit Éclaireur.*

I had not relighted my fire. I had not hoisted my flag. Today I was afraid of men. Instinctively I protected myself against the hundred million enemies of whose existence I was learning. I had, in an instant, almost without thinking of it, camouflaged this island which from my mere presence had assumed a certain French life and aspect: now nothing on it could have exasperated the captain of German corsair. By sunflower seeds I drew all the parrots who spoke French to the centre of the island, and the shore was freed of them . . . I could read the *Petit Eclaireur* only line by line, with rests in be-

tween, for reading was a torture to my eyes. I
held in check all that I had thought until now
regarding good and evil, all my logic, all my
tastes and my distastes, determined to decide in
favor of my country. If my country had attacked
Germany, surprised her frontier, violated Belgium,
I permitted the sudden expansion of the tiny base
nerve in my soul which sanctions the violation of
Belgium. If the French had pillaged, had violated, I
lifted that latch—slightly rusty—in my brain which
approves the pillage and violation of the Palatinate.
If the French had fled, I loosed the demon of rout;
that astonishing love for ambulances overturned in
the mud, for dogs killed by the bayonet blow of
an enfeebled corporal, that taste for mutinies against
the officer who bars the road,—I let this demon—so
feeble in young girls' hearts—expand within me.
If the English, their fleet sunk, were barring the
sea by nets and submarines, I sanctioned that wrinkle
in my heart which permits cruel shipwrecks. Already all these evil elements, microscopic as yet,
were opposed in me to those great sad and pure
forms (always full-size in young girls' souls)—the
conquest of Alsace by trumpets, the kindness of
Zouaves to their prisoners, the anarchist and the
royalist helping each other to the hospital,—forms

suddenly motionless and bloodless which awaited a
word from me to be revitalized.

But already I had read the larger headlines, and
then the medium-sized ones. Already I knew that
Kipling's son had been killed and that the nephew
of M. Boilard, chief customs officer of Shanghai,
had been killed also: the only two whose names I
knew; statistics told me that there were eight
million dead in Europe. I felt all the sadness, especially all the remorse, that such news evokes . . .
However, I counted for so little in it all! In what
way did I share in the responsibility for so much
horror! Why did I feel slightly guilty? What
former movements of mine, what words, had
thrown a weight, however light, in the scale of war?
In what way had I been lacking in prudence, in
the days at Bellac, and rested my weight upon the
scale? All the trees in Picardy cut down, said a
headline. No more horses in France, said another.
In what way had I led a tree or a French horse to
death? Yes, I had neglected on the two occasions that I had dealt directly with Germany herself
to coax her or to draw her on. I had spoken badly
of Werther; at school I had found him more of
a liar than a sensualist, more middle-class than
upper-class. And, on another occasion, I had

indicated to a German in his Mercédes the road to
Limoges when he had inquired the road to Poitiers.
He had seen Saint-Martial instead of Saint-Rade-
gonde. That was my humble share in this war: I
had turned against us the shade of Werther and a
reserve captain . . .

I read. I read obscure pages. I saw France led
by unknown names: Joffre, Pétain. I saw that there
was a daily *communiqué*, and that only the 911th
had come to me. I learned that that great boat, the
only one on which I had formerly depended, the
Lusitania, was sunk; I discovered that they were
killing in aeroplanes, that they were launching gas.
I had a four column description of the expulsion of
M. Dahlen from the German school at Shanghai;
all details regarding Siam's fidelity to the Allies,
and the devotion of Cochin China; the names of
all the patronesses of the charity fête at Hanoi; the
names of all the passengers and native Macaoans
sunk on the Tokyohara. I learned that the high
admiral lived ashore, the General-in-Chief in a
pinnace. I would have been able to understand this
war perfectly had there not been in every article an
insoluble phrase which always contained the name
of the same river, having no apparent connection
with the subject. "The Germans are in France,"

said the first journalist, "but what have they to say
about the Marne," "Few grapes in France this year,"
said the second, "the Marne will suffice for Frenchmen." On the literary page they consoled themselves for the atrocities of the cubists with the same
counterbalance: "We have visited the Indepen-
dents," said the critic, M. Clapier, "happily there is
the Marne," . . . It even frightened me a little to
see my country defended against the Germans and
against bad art by this one word as by a talisman.
What if the word Marne became void, outworn,
and France and the Academy were without arms!
It was a word which seemed valuable in other
countries also, the sole French money whose exchange rate had not fallen: "Brazil is stripped of
india-rubber," said the financial page, "it finds consolation in the Marne." And not a single journalist who slipped and said: "Greece is unfaithful, but
there is the Saône." "French architects are nil, but
there is the Vire . . . " Under every line of the
Petit Éclaireur the one name Marne ran like a
stream beneath the separated planks of a bridge. So
strong was the influence that I mechanically said
aloud, trying this balm on myself: "She is alone
on her island, but there is the Marne . . . " And
in truth, the Marne suddenly promised me my re-

turn, so clearly did I once more see that fisherman with his enchanted line at the river's mouth at Charenton: I had complimented him and he had given me his left hand, shaking as much of that sacred water as possible from his fish with his right hand in order not to wet his pocket too much . . .

A sparrow, tamed no doubt on one of the sunken ships—sparrows are assuredly ugly and common, but there is the Marne—came to light on my shoulder and did not desert me.

CHAPTER IX

"My dear Simon:

"First a two line summing-up to put you *au courant*. I am not dead, but Polynesian. I have protected my island from an alligator and a cougar. I have refused, despite solicitations, to be my own idol. I maintain a troop composed of two hundred and thirty-three gods and the phantoms of eighteen men. An ornithorhynchus, on which is perched the laziest of my birds, dogs my heels. I am writing you because I found a case full of fountain-pens in the pocket of a drowned sailor named Rudolf Eberlein, and because ink evaporates . . . Now you know everything.

"I am writing you from a headland that I have decorated with a thousand circlets of pearl-shell, as they do with the gas-lamps and refuges in London from which one signals automobiles. I am visible every day from two o'clock until six at least. I might even say that no human being in the world has ever been more visible: on a tripod at either side of me pine cones are burning to create two smoke columns; a curtain of red feathers three metres high is stretched from the palm tree at my left to the palm tree at my right; the paving is of black coral; and can't you guess, too, from these few lines (you get the same impression from them that you sometimes experience in talking to a girl over the telephone, who admits it, no more than I) that I am writing you naked? I have a ruled sheet of paper on my knees, and through it I can feel the running pen which pricks me so pleasantly at the periods and commas that I am going to multiply the short phrases . . . The sky . . . The sea . . . The sky is either all sparkling or all red: here it is always the end of a great fire; the black butterflies flutter about, powerless in space, exactly like pieces of burned paper; the sea on the reef is the cooling kettle; the palms clack like tongs. The world has burned and I, warm, am its poor residue.

"All is luxury here, Simon. Long birds with vermilion tails climb the abysses of light at a leap—as salmon climb waterfalls—up to the light of the sun from which they are born, their tails taking new life from a ray. Each bush, was doubtless so surprised by me that since my shipwreck it has borne the fruit of another. Here the apple trees give oranges, the fig trees cherries. Here is a world where flowers, birds, animals and insects, mingled in happiness, have not had time since my arrival to recover their attributes: hairy beasts lay eggs; fish set. Everything that poets alone can see in France, one sees here with the naked eye: the trees drink from the sea by real trunks which contract when it is too salt. All that is said in antiphrasis of Parisian women could be said truly of me: my complexion is pearly, powdered with real pearl; my lips are coral, powdered with real coral. The colors, also, have been put on again too quickly: the leaves are carmine or purple; the fruits are green as soon as they are ripe.

"Here without any trouble one can have all your European sounds and perfumes. To hear the noise of poplars I need only close my eyes, lie down in the submarine cave, and listen to the noise of the sea on the pebbles. In order to hear a murmuring like that of a mass, with clacking *prie-Dieu,* I have only to stay awake at night where the big bustards make their nests. To hear the clarion or the sound of the sledge-hammer that is wielded at the fairs by the contestants for a medal, it is enough to fasten a goose to an old decaying tree. It would deceive anyone. There is even a noise which not only replaces the other but which is the same, and I listen to it as often as possible, for it recalls Bellac and the plush chimney-piece: the noise of a hollow shell at my ear. And to see once again certain movements which are habitual at home is scarcely more difficult. In order to re-discover your yellow glove which I used to see on the banister, without seeing yourself, when you went down past my fourth floor, I have only to lean over the lagoon and follow a yellow trout that regains the bottom in circles which grow steadily smaller. As for the gesture of the conductor who rings the bell to tell you that the tram is full, I have two monkeys who make it when I approach their palm tree. It is just like Europe. There are mornings, too, when I am tired out; not with the weariness of one who has been fanned by the monsoon or washed by the Kuro Siwo three times a day, but like one who has spent the

preceding evening with his feet braced against a
stair-case, whose shoulders are bent from having
traveled standing up in a belt-line train.   Here, before
this island which has become a mirror for my soul
and which I confuse with it; before these *dalagan-
palangs* which resemble a caprice that I have had, this
Bahiki hill with red and black hollows that exactly
counterfeits a slight pain that I feel, these sluggish
birds who imitate to perfection the dust of thought
which flies around my thought; I, the queen, am suddenly oppressed by my perfection and wish that my
body were as awkward as it was in Bellac when it
broke the twelfth glass of each service; I wish my
ear were polluted; I would like to be told; 'talk to someone, recollect something'; I would like to hear Madame
Blebé call her girls her "young ladies"; I am tired of
these invisible hooks that prevent me from falling from
the highest trees, of these air-pockets within me that
support me in the waters' depths; I would like to
touch a drunken man, a typhus patient; and, when
night comes, I forget to light my fires of sandalwood
and to command from my over-perfumed island the
winking that will one day attract a roving ship.

"Alone, Simon: and, nevertheless, I feel the irritation of all those places in my body which were sensible
only to contacts with men.   That tickling in my hip,
which used to seize me as soon as a blond man whis-
pered in my ear, is now a real sensation, a real scar.
I feel again that weakness in my shoulders which used
to come from a dark young man speaking to me of
the theatre.   That little finger of my left hand which
used to move tirelessly when a slightly frivolous woman

held out her right hand to me,—it moves . . . And
someone simultaneously crossed all those fords in my
body yesterday when I decided to blow up with cartridges found on a German sailor the stone hiding
place of the unknown man who preceded me in the
second island. Deafened by the explosion—like their
brothers the fish when one fishes with dynamite—the
birds remained cowering all around, and then for the
first time I could seize the wildest bird in the island.
I thrust my arm through the open crack in the wall,
placing the paradise bird beside me like a package.
Ungluing them from the bony structure of the island
as from a binding, I withdrew some book pages. Like
a big boarding school girl slipping notes to the smaller
one she adores through the crack of her door, this
dead man passed me some French poems and some
pages from novels. He was some brave conscientious
explorer who believed that one really should carry
around the world those ten masterpieces which the
Annales caused to be chosen by plebiscite: page 31 of
Don Quixote; page 214 of Montaigne; 69 of *Jaques le
Fataliste*. I read each page immediately, more disconsolate when I discovered I had read the verso before
the recto than I used to be when some one told me
the end of a novel in advance; finding a beginning, a
middle, and a conclusion to each one of these isolated
passages on the gait of Rosinante, on the theft of a
purse by Jaques, on egoism; and I was as full after
eight pages as though I had read eight novels. Page
180 of La Rochefoucauld on women, which distressed
me, in which he had foreseen everything, excepting my
case, in which he unjustly railed at my paints and

powders and my fidelity, and showed me old age coming from Europe to rejoin me in the island. Page 55 of *Gil Blas,* which alone recalled many names to me: judges, mules, duennas, and the ghostly cavalier. But, without mentioning names, it was above all a pack of adverbs, conjunctions and exclamations which came back to me, and I felt my soul rejuvenated by them like an old cushion with new springs. I stuffed my thought with them; I separated by them all the words which little by little had been joined together in my phrases; I resolved to speak in the presence of the echo with 'whether . . . or,' 'according as,' and 'althoughs.' After each page I thrust my hand afresh into the cavern, resting my free hand on the paradise bird which had recovered its senses and was struggling and pecking at me, finally liberating him as ransom for a volume which I withdrew almost intact, and whose title was such that I remained motionless for a moment as above a mirror: Robinson Crusoe!

"A beggar understands his misfortune only in seeing a beggar, a negro a negro, a dead man only when he sees a dead man. Because of egotism the idea of comparing my lot with that of Robinson's had never come to me until today. I had not wished to admit that his frightful solitude was my own. The sight of that second island, round like a balloon, above my island, had kept my hope alive. But today I thumbed the book like a medical manual on a disease that one suddenly believes is one's own . . . It was surely mine . . . the same symptoms, the same words . . . birds, beasts; a little land surrounded on all sides by water

. . . Night was falling; I lighted two torches . . .
Alone, alone on the fringe of an archipelago, a woman
was going to read Robinson Crusoe.

"I read until morning, until the hour when the big-
gest stars are heaped together in a corner of the sky beside a heavenly winner, and when my tame ptemerops
flew around my head in unvarying circles as around a
coffee-grinder, whose grating was his cry . . . But I,
seeking precepts, advice, and examples in this book,
was stupefied at the few lessons that my senior
could give me.   First of all, he was a German
from Bremen, named Kreuzer: I was a little disappointed at this, like an American jailor who finds a
negro or a Chinaman in the cell in which he has locked
up a superb Irishman.   Then, perhaps because of the
lack of faith which his origin gave me, I found him
a whiner, and incoherent.   This Puritan who was
loaded down with rationality, with the certainty that
he was the unique toy of Providence, did not confide
himself to her for a single minute.   Every instant for
eighteen years—as though he were always on his raft
—he was fastening cords, sawing stakes, and nailing
planks.   This bold man was constantly trembling with
fear, and it was thirteen years before he dared to
reconnoitre all his island.   This sailor who from his
promontory could see with his naked eye the mists
of a continent never thought of starting toward it,
while I had swum all round my archipelago at the
end of a few months.   Clumsy, hollowing out boats in
the center of the island; always walking the Equator
with parasols as on a tight rope.   Meticulous, knowing
all the names of the most useless European objects

15

and not resting until he had learned all trades. He required a table to eat, a chair to write, wheelbarrows, ten kinds of baskets (and he despaired at not achieving the eleventh), more provision bags than a housekeeper would want on market-day, three kinds of sickles and scythes, and a sieve, and a grindstone, and a harrow, and a mortar, and a sifter. And jars, square, oval and round; and porringers; and a Brot mirror; and all varieties of stew-pans. Already encumbering his poor island as his nation was later to encumber the world with shop-made goods and tin-plate. The book was full of pictures, not a single one of which showed him at rest: it was Robinson digging, or sewing, or fixing eleven guns in a loop-holed wall, or setting up a scare-crow to frighten away birds. Always busy, not as though he were separated from mankind but as if he were embroiled with them, and knowing neither of the two perils of solitude: suicide and madness. He was perhaps the one man—so superstitious and such a busy-body did I find him—that I would have not liked to meet on an island. Never burning his fortress in an enthusiasm for God, never dreaming of a woman, devoid of divination, and without instinct. So it was I who took the floor to give him advice at each moment, to say to him: 'Turn to the left, turn to the right.' To tell him: 'Sit down there; put down your parasol, your gun and your cane. You are on a headland, parrots are flying all around you; then write some verses. Why the devil don't you come from Dusseldorf instead of Bremen! Don't work three months to make yourself a table: squat. Don't lose six months in making yourself a *prie-Dieu*: kneel down

there. Don't find a way of having cave-ins as in a
mining country, or electrical accidents as in a future
century. What's the difference if you don't succeed
in perfecting the springs that hold your umbrella and
your parasol closed? Leave them all open at the door
of the forests or you won't be able to go in with them.
Think rather of me, who to play you a trick would
press on the sand of your island with my hand, not
my foot, and then disappear. What the devil would
you say about that woman's hand! That tree that
you want to cut down to plant your barley,—shake
it. It's a palm tree; it will give you bread ready baked.
That other that you are pulling up to sew peas,—gather
those yellow snakes on it that are called bananas; peel
them. I love you, in spite of all, you who speak of
the taste of every bird on the island and never of his
song. What would you say to a glass of beer?'

"Thus I read all night long, until the hour when
Friday, quite black, arrived with the morning. The
moon was setting. At times (was it a pearl taking a
skin at the bottom of the lagoon?) the whole sea bulged
and became opaline. The Great Bear was folded up
before me like a carpenter's rule,—my poor island too
small for such a measure . . . It was not an Oceanic
silence, but that of a station when the last train has
left, and the sea on the reefs played the vanishing
train, and a cocoanut fell with the noise of a signal-
disk, and with my foot caught in a creeper I did not
dare to move as if I might disturb a switch . . . All
that little feminine energy which had been minutely
constructed in my cranium like a ship in a bottle fell
into fragments at the mere word Friday. Friday

plunged into me, to my very heart, by a shorter road than that of a pearl diver. Everything that Friday thought seemed natural to me; what he did, useful: no advice to give him. I understood that taste for human flesh which he retained for several months. I felt that his slightest step away from Robinson's beaten track had led me to a spring or to a treasure; and everything that this Kreuzer maniac had spent years in accomplishing became justified by Friday's presence. How nice, in truth, it must have been to show Friday the beautiful stone hedge, to teach him to shell beans in jar number four; to reveal to him how the umbrella closed and opened; how one made the roast turn by a system of six spits and two strings. And God, how he turns and turns away? And the Trinity, how it is three and one? To teach immortality to Friday, your eyes in his eyes, and to breathe it into his very mouth, like life into a drowned man; to enjoy his first triumph over the mortal animals and trees, to see his hand pityingly stroke the baobab which will die in a thousand years. And my thirty metre screens, and my tamed animals,—what torture, Simon, not to be assured that I can some day show them to some one! To someone who is hurrying a little. For I feel, as too many feathers fall, as too much hair grows, that the year will come when my parrots will be a hundred years old, my gazelles twelve, and they will commence to die.

"So you see, Simon, (for I insist on ending my letter by a conceit; they ordered us to do it at school) that the saddest day in my island was the one when I was joined by Robinson.

"Farewell.   Write me what's going on in Europe."

.   .   .   .

Simon answered me the same evening, in a letter written by my hand, that the news of Europe was that the war was ending.   The uniform was now garnet with red epaulettes.   He had been the first to enter Strasbourg on the anniversary of Bazeilles, and on the anniversary of Sedan we had taken Berlin.

He added some phrases which, simple as they were, moved me almost as much : that the *Printemps* was having its duvetine exposition; that the Saint-Lazare station omnibus had become an autobus; that the messenger boy at Larue's was wearing crepe on his arm.   All the habitués were wringing his hand.

Then he told me some other things, still more simple, but with the air of relating curious anecdotes : that people were loving, people were hating, people were meeting at stations, people were marrying and living together.

Then, some lines on trades which appeared still stranger to me : that tile-works were making tiles, grocers groceries, pastry-cooks pastry . . .

.   .   .   .

I answered him :

"Dear Simon :

"Now all the oysters and all the clams around my island are closing with the noise of bayonets being thrust back into their scabbards.   Now is the hour

when they used to tell me that the sun was sinking
into the sea, that the sun was taking its bath: I used
to say nothing; I had always considered it so much
more than that!

I am escaping from a great danger. Since yesterday
morning I have no longer been balanced in my island
between two worlds, as in the basket of a balloon,
with birds and plants given to me without names and
without conditions. In the note-book of the shipwrecked man across the way I have found the plan of
my archipelago, its latitude, and the exact number of
miles that separate it from Palmyra Island (770),
from Rimsky Korsakoff Island (321) and from Raka-
kanga (exactly 1,000). It was almost as though my
wandering life on my raft were finished. I felt myself
held by cables to the four corners of the horizon.
From these maps I could learn, almost to a metre,
the depth of each hole in my sea. All those trees that
I had baptized were catalogued and sketched in this
note-book according to their species; and little by
little their beautiful pseudonyms were replaced by their
vulgar or Latin names. I had no more balsams, baobabs, and choke-pears, but sagos and nutmegs; my
cocoanut tree was only the *palmier pincette;* my little
red and green shrub was an indigo plant; my big yellow
apples were only meagre catechus. Science was going
to alight on this round spot in the middle of the Pacific
and drink it up like a blotter. My birds were going
to put on the uniforms they wore at the Jardin des
Plantes. Alas! some were even drawn: my favorite
yellow one was a male tarin; my black-bird fan was a
kind of fly-catcher; my parrot who changed his feathers

and color every month was a bee-eater. The shipwrecked man specified that to recognize any species
of bird it was merely necessary to inspect their irises,
and in spite of myself I looked those who alighted in
the eye. One, whose iris was composed of two circles,
the largest blue, the smallest brown, was the Papuan
lory. Another, whose iris was blood-red with a golden
centre, was the *combattant troupiale*. Another, who
was squint-eyed, was the Dupont bird of paradise.
And two wash-drawing plates did not permit me to
be ignorant any longer of the name of a single shell:
thenceforward I trod on bits of ammonite nautilus,
and limpet. It was enough for me to read and to
accept this contract in order to annex all this inde-
pendent flora and fauna to the rest of the world, to
Buffon and to Cuvier. Like a tender on a tow-line,
I felt myself hitched on to your train for an instant.
Latin winds, English winds, a Netherland's summer
breeze: that was what my monsoon and my twelve
trade-winds were. I hesitated no longer; as you burn,
without reading them, the letters that tell you of an
old love of one whom you thought pure, I threw the
inventory into the fire; I freed my birds and my fish
from their past, and as for the stupid name of the
island, I don't even wish to tell it to you,—I want to
forget it.

"Don't be disturbed at my orthography. It requires
more than a slight effort, after five years, to hold my
pen to double letttttttters!

"Today I am calmer. What calms me above all,
when I am writing, is to trace a word in large capitals.
I am CALM. Why don't you writers in France

employ this procedure? This CALM, as though one suddenly had a magnifying-glass before one's eyes. Let us try, in order to see if the cure is really sure, to write a word that pains me: the word station; the word wardrobe, the word CHENONCEAUX.

"Don't tell me that you love me. You imagine me long since diluted in the sea; perhaps, at most, you imagine that a bit of me has penetrated into thoroughly yellow creatures, and you caress them . . . Nevertheless, you who have Chenonceaux, Chambord and Valencay, love me . . .

"Don't tell me that you are dying without me. You are dying without uttering my name, without looking into my eyes to discover therein—like the shipwrecked man in the birds' irises—my true species . . . However, you who are over there, you who have the papers, the *Figaro,* the *Matin, l'Echo* and the *Débats,* you who can get by return courier *la Gazette de Limoges,* love me . . .

"Ah! Simon. Like a chemist who stops all at once in making up a prescription and divines suddenly, without reason, that his vocation was to be a geometer, like a jockey who, holding King's-Dragon by the bridle, had a sudden revelation that he was born for medicine, so I at this moment, and without reason, divine that I was made for LOVE, for LOVE.

"For love at Chamounix: I see the window of the hotel room for which I was created. For love at Saint-Moritz: I see the skiers. How stupid one is in life! I think that snow is a solid, that, despite everything, it should make a light noise in falling, yet I never thought of listening to it. I think that all those human beings around me who were loving each other must have been clasping their hands passionately, hugging in the bay-windows; crying . . . and I never noticed or heard anything. During my twenty years in the world, nothing that would allow me to believe that people were loving. Tell me what you were doing with Anne, Simon. Tell me without lying!"

.   .   .   .

Simon replied that he was going to tell me everything. When he was with Anne they were kissing. Very often, behind my back. There had been no silence, for the one who was not kissing had continued to speak. He had stretched her out on my rose divan in the hotel, quickly, while I was preparing tea. The sound of steps that had astonished me was their four feet finding the floor again, it was they getting up. He was bending over her and that cry, which he had partially covered up by overturning the waste receptacle of hammered copper, that cry which had made me come running all pale, and which I had stupidly believed was a cry of fright, as if cause followed effect, was . . .

Here I tore up his letter.

.   .   .   .

"Dear Simon:

"Alas! Yes, I have come to the point of saying out loud when a white cloud suddenly rises up: 'The train is leaving!' and of shouting at times, when I am hungry: 'To table!'

"It is to escape these dolorous visits of French words that I have acquired the habit of making words for myself and that I now have a language of my own. I have stripped the trees and birds of even those deformed European names with which I tricked them out at random, as a Senegambian king puts on a stove-pipe hat and corsets. No more plum-cocoanuts, *adonisiers, kerikerisiers.* I have a full two hundred words that never carry me outside the island in which they were born, not even those which signify Nostalgia or Waiting.

"It is a fluid language, for lazy as I always am I have spared myself the trouble of including in it x's and nasals. No more of those aspirate h's which I have always detested, that stick the word to your face like an ether mask. A language without suffixes, prefixes or roots, in which the most similar creatures have the most dissimilar names. Whistling names, invariably followed by a beautiful epithet that feeds them like a coal-car. Rolling names, many of which I forge before the echo, shouting them and modifying them until an unalloyed name comes back to me from the rock . . . Glaia: the feeling one has when all the red leaves of the mango are turned back by the wind and become white. Kirara: the soul movement when the thousand bats which have been hanging to a dead tree like figs detach themselves one by one. Hiroza: when they all start off together and catch a bird in their group. Ibili: the meeting with a creeper which has slid down to the beach, that could be linked up with a cable. Koiva: for all the movements of the human arm; and identical names for the most diverse desires. Azie:

for that caress of a bird's wings which I feel incessantly, and for love.   I am Veloa, the Queen, and
I must not be confused with Velloa, the lack of black-
currants and quince brandy.   Then, in order to be less
alone, I make all the most feminine words of the old
world masculine: the sea, the earth, and the night have
become beings of another sex than mine.   The moon
is Sikole, female for four days, male for three.   Try
to imagine, too, that the mango, the cherry, and the
pear change gender while you approach them with
your lips.   The other day I compared my vocabulary
with the dictionary of the neighboring islands, found
in the grotto.   On one object—one only, but the most
precious in the Pacific—on the word for sun, I found
myself in agreement with their real language.   I am
very proud of it.   For happy is he who guesses the
Esquimaux word which means Ice, the English word
which means Marmalade, the French word which means
Honor . . .

"My battle against solitude?   Sometimes I fight it
by swimming to the island of the gods, by shaking
their tiny hands, by caressing their immense lips, and
by standing motionless in the place from which one
of them is missing, replacing a god *ad interim*.   Sometimes by planting the island with scarecrows, which,
however, never frighten away the birds, their outer
wrapping being of feathers.   At times by using my
shadow to make all the movements of friends that
can be imagined, all poses of famous statues, all profiles,
—the one poor cinema that gives me a European
spectacle.   I try them on the sand by sunlight or on
the pearl-shell by moonlight, with a banana peel on

my nose to form Montespan's shadow. I amuse myself, too, by being two women successively. Today a person who walks backward through the forests, stirring up springs and breaking eggs. Tomorrow, another person who follows the valleys, dwells in the glades, carrying the five senses of the island, united on her narrow countenance, only to spots cherished by the sun. Each one true to her name.

"The first is always naked; the second harnessed with orchids. But I am these two, alas! only by turns. Like those heroines who play the double rôle of twins in the movies, it is only by artifice that they can meet and just touch each other with their fingers to change places at midnight. One is capable of all exploits, the other of all baseness. The one is idolatrous, credulous; the other reasons. The one has a tendency to grow fat; the other to grow thin. The one walks on the balls of her feet; the other on her heels; and they do not leave the same tracks in the island. The one is innocent, the other perverse; and their mouths do not leave the same marks on the fruit. One caresses the foreheads of the animals; the other strokes them. In fine, in perfecting them I have simply arrived at separating them, as Dominic did formerly, and nothing less than a good sting from a wasp or cactus will solder my soul and my body together again for a moment. I live, therefore, on one foot.

"My soul is something very slight, very common, and I have never perceived in it even the shadow of a stranger. I have pulled in vain on those little ends of cruelty and of anger which formerly gave me the illusion that I might be pitiless and sanguinary at need.

I have tried to strangle the tango bird, in order to know the limits of impassibility: it has had confidence in me, and has died some weeks later to prove that it could die only from disillusionment. My soul is a nice girl. But around my body, powdered and stretched out motionless on a manchineel like bait, I sometimes feel Polynesian spirits roaming. I paint it so that it will show me an unrecognizable aspect in the water. I hide it; I bury it under leaves; I fasten it to a tree by creepers of its own color; I know all the places in the island where it secretly lodges. What European explorer could discover me at these times, when I am the best hidden woman in the world! Often, too, I sleep on that moss which colors one red. I arise with one half of me colored for the week, cut in two by a capricious line, rich in beautiful dove-tails that I accentuate with the color. I have two dissimilar hands, unequal legs; each feature is alien to the other; and if I pray, and if I cross my knees, half-person that I am, at least I am living with a half-person who is less familiar.

"How do I still busy myself, Simon? I wait.

"It is my one work, a real work that I cannot neglect for a morning or an afternoon without feeling the same remorse that idleness gives us at home: I wait. It is my trade. Stretched out or seated before the sea, I wait. I am no longer anything but an eye; I have reached the stage of not winking it that I may not lose the thousandth of a chance. My whole sky, my whole sea is spread like a spider's web, and I am ready to spring on the bark that will be caught in it. Sometimes, at most, two birds which have been flying in company

separate from each other suddenly; I feel my glance
ripped apart, and I have to shut my eyes for a second.
Or I have to roll them at times in order to shake up
two irises suddenly widened by two vague twins.
Without a single thought—like the young girls who
wait on terraces for one of those French sentiments to
which a little complacency at evening would give
human form—I wait for a man. I am not waiting
for one of those transatlantic liners that carry
men to mediocre fates, but for the two most different skiffs imaginable, which carry the most widely
separated beings; a pirogue, first of all; or, on
the contrary, a yacht. I am at the cross-roads of the
most refined happiness and the iron age. Instead of
the feeble deviation which the needle makes for young
girls in France, between an officer and a civil servant,
it makes a complete circle here: a millionaire or a
savage. I no longer feel myself balanced between a
red haired man and a brunette, between a little fellow
with a gymnast's belt who prefers Bordeaux and a big
chap with a checkered scarf who prefers Burgundy;
but between two races separated by twenty thousand
years, between the youth and age of the world, between
a grass bed on the third floor right of a giant tree,
with a tame panther on the landing and hollow skulls
for bells, and all the linen and silk of New York;—if,
on the other hand, a man does not arrive from the
convict island that they tell me is nearby; an escaped
prisoner with hard-boiled eggs wrapped up in news-
papers . . . Would I prefer death to life with a
savage? A savage whom I would never *tutoyer,* to
whom, in fine, I would accord, in the eyes of his

brothers, that demi-divinity which I refuse to the demons of the island, who would truly believe that I gave him immortality, and whom, on the day of his death (this would be the hardest) I would pretend to love no longer and to punish? . . . And that polished Englishman who would say, holding out his hand to me, quite naked, for our first hand-shake: 'Will you pardon my glove?' And that American pastor who would quickly photograph me with his university flag for a dress? And that German, overflowing with love, who would install me at a folding table in front of Pilsener beer, condemning me to a kiss every time I forgot to close the pewter cap of the glass?

"On the days when I feel too keenly that the gentlemen of the world have not started the race toward me, I wait for the wind . . .

"As in an auto one can tell by simply looking at a little red tube in front of one, or at a little blue tube at the left, whether it has its oil or gasoline, so I now know the tiny objects on this island which can tell me whether it has its fill of sun or wind. I know all the details of the Pacific machinery. If that silver spangle in a hole on the left hand corner of rock Rimbaud glitters, it means that the moon is full. That sliver of the fallen tree suddenly turning the color of ox-blood means rain for the day after tomorrow. Those bees coming out of the top of the tree mean an earthquake for the beginning of the following day. That water lily moving three times (it is the rarest phenomenon; almost annual) means the passage of the ornithorhynchus across the island. So I have only to watch certain shadows, certain glitterings, like taxi-metres, in order to know if the wind, the monsoon, or the tempest are coming toward me. It is enough for me to cast my eyes on a palm leaf, which an ignorant person could not distinguish from its fellows but which is my manometre, the only one that trembles an hour before the slightest breeze. I consult it constantly, disappointed when it remains motionless for too many days . . . Suddenly it shivers . . . From the sea in which I am bathing I hoist myself up onto the platform of the headland: in the same way that I used to tell the direction of the wind with a moistened finger when I was a little girl, I use my whole body to tell it up there. It comes in squalls, attacking my caressing side or my implacable side according to the time of year; brutally pressing on me first of all, on sterile me, the greediest of those perfumes and invisible seeds that would be so fruitful were I earth instead of flesh. Protesting wind, suddenly plastering me with an entire leaf of unknown shape; it arrives tenderly, licking me in waves, sometimes from above as through an open studio window, or from below as through a heat register in a museum. Then the bird who announces the end of the wind utters his cry, a cry that is almost imperceptible in the midst of warblings; the wave which announces the swell for 12:15 A.M. covers me with spume; the heron, which flies away thirty-five minutes before the day's close, rises; not a breath; the complete obscurity which announces night envelops me, and I despair on my broken-down island . . .

"One keeps busy, alone on an island! . . ."

CHAPTER X

I HAD been awakened abruptly; but by what? By a dream? Or, rather, had a cannon thundered during the last second of my sleep; had I not been illumined by a searchlight? I was scrutinizing, all at once, in order to discover the cause of this start, my mind, my body, and the horizon. I was groping about in the darkened island, leaning on my most sensitive birds, bumping against hollow trees, calling the echo, like a person seeking the electric button in a drawing room. I succeeded only in making the sun get up. From the depths of my cave at last —like a person who, having lost a ring, turns the whole house upside down, sits down on the last chair where he still had it, thinks, gets up, and goes straight to the right drawer—I rushed out, climbed the nearest cocoanut tree, and sought the smoke of the geyser in the other island . . . I had found it . . . Two columns of smoke were rising.

It was not a mirage. There were two smokes, and not four islands, not two lines of breakers. On that still fresh dawn I saw the breath of men imprint itself . . . Men were still living . . . If I had had better eyes I might, perhaps have been able to see a third smoke, very small,—that of a cigarette or a pipe! . . . I was suddenly inert at the top of my cocoanut tree, as if I had been holding myself there for five years; a few minutes more and I could have borne solitude no longer; had the smoke appeared at eight o'clock, not at seven, it would have been too late: I would have let go entirely. So strong was this feeling that I really let go of the tree, and fell, the ripest of its fruits . . . I was at the edge of the sea; I threw myself into the Kuro Siwo as into a taxi.

Today I was too light for this salt water. At times I came out of it almost entirely. I held myself down, and made myself heavy, fearing they would see from the other bank. The shipwrecked man's book had revealed to me the races and customs of the neighboring archipelagos, and there was enough to make me distrustful. If the west wind had blown during the night, the new arrival came from Haühaü, where they deify white men. But if it had blown from the East, he came from Meyer Island where they eat them stuffed; and the north wind would bring him

from Samua Bay where the Papuans cut off their
heads. I held my arm clear of the water to see
whence came this wind that was going to make me
a slave or a queen. There was not a breath; the
smoke columns were rising perfectly straight; my
visitor came from the centre of the earth. My
visitor (the idea suddenly struck me) had come in
a steam-yacht. But I was then frightened by the
awkwardness of Europeans: they were capable of
mistaking me for a shark, from the swell in the
water, and of shooting. I was trying in vain—for
they were also capable of firing on it with a shot-
gun—to drive away the cloud of parrots who were
flying just above me, speaking my language and
disclosing my presence. Suddenly, like a child's
balloon that I had released, this cloud rose . . .
The stranger must have made a move. Then, from
the second island, I saw sheafs of red paradise birds
climbing, then rose ones, then violet; someone was
stirring this fine fire; the stranger must have fired;
but I was already near the breakers, and with my
right ear to the sea, like a shell, I could hear nothing
but the sea. At last I was in the lagoon, and I
heard a bleating, then a yelping: the stranger must
have seized my deer by his horns, my monkey by
his tail. The fish in this still water were frightened

also. Not one of them stayed in the depth of
his own color—the rose ablets on coral, the tench
over striate depths—but, mistakenly thinking they
could win security by changing their background,
the golden ones swam above pearl, the green ones
over white sand. All were agitated by a regular
movement that pushed them forward a millimetre a second; and before long, in truth, I
heard the noise of a motor . . . Too late . . .
For at the instant my foot touched land I saw
a gasoline launch take the passage between the
reefs and swiftly head straight toward my island.
I was playing puss-in-the-corner for more than
my life. I watched them go, feeling hate for
the first time, dripping, with not a dry spot on me
save my eyes . . . Suddenly the tears gushed from
them . . .

A man's glance! I had seen a man's glance! A
man's glance had touched me, without seeing me,
as the searchlight had before! In a sunburned
face—as unskilful at hiding themselves as the fish
had just been—two blue eyes! That was all: the
edge of the launch cut the head just below. I had
not seen a human nose, a human mouth. The chin,
the neck, the shoulders,—I had seen nothing of all
those. But I had seen eyebrows, a forehead, ears.

I had seen black bushy hair. I had not seen those
eyelids wink, for everything had been too rapid; but
I had seen a hand lifted from the launch to caress
that hair, and another hand that touched the ear
gently. A man, all complete, was there, every part
of whose body caressed the others!

At this moment I caught sight of a coat hanging
from a tree. The breeze had come up, an east
breeze, bringing too late the cook who was going to
roast me; but it was stirring this vestment and putting it through puppet movements that immediately
recalled to me, as though I had forgotten them,
all the movements of men. The arm was swing-
ing, the neck was opening; it was the coat of a
walking, breathing man. I fingered it; I plucked
it at the very point at which it was fastened to
the tree, in order not to damage it, like a fruit.
I was sure they would come back to look for
it; it was not the kind of a coat that one abandons in an island: it was one of those masterpieces
in white and brown homespun for which one would
not hesitate to disturb, at evening, the woman who
was seated on it and already asleep. Lined with
grey-brown silk, it was adorable, with cuffs on the
sleeves and a martingale. But they would not find it
without me, for I was enveloped in it! Like

Oriental lovers in the harem rugs;—they could not take it back without me to Mr. Billy Kinley, who was its master according to the label. I attached myself to everything that it contained. About my wrist I knotted a gold and gray silk handkerchief that smelled of benzoin; at my knee a handkerchief of green silk that smelled of bergamot. With two masculine perfumes, I made myself two moorings. I rummaged the pockets, eager to touch at last the residue of a world that a man carries on himself: all were empty. But at least each had its odor: one smelled of tobacco, the other of chocolate, the little breast pocket of menthol. I breathed these salt cellars; after five years I was restored to life; Europe with its perfumes passed by my door . . . I flung myself toward my echoes in order to shout there the call that I had so often rehearsed to them; I ran to the quadruple echo, disdaining the double and the triple; the wind had turned and was coming from the west. Too late, for what did I care now about being a goddess at Haühaü! I was running, frightening my armadillos which sought their burrows anew and my monkeys, climbing their trees again. The animals left me the whole ground for this human interview . . . I was at the centre of the small, almost round island, when I saw the launch approaching once more, doubtless in search of me. The man shouted. Then, among the cocoanut trees on my right, I heard another man singing. Then, far behind me, a banjo. A fourth man was whistling near the sea. Simultaneously I heard the four harmonies of which human beings are capable. And, on the instant that my echo had rejected my appeal four times, I felt this circumference closing in; my solitude was assaulted by four men with guns, revolvers, and hatchets; already branches were cracking, and suddenly, when the human pressure grew too great for me—twenty metres, thirty metres; so sensitive had I become—don't faint Suzanne! —I fainted . . .

.   .   .   .

I decided that I would neither budge nor reopen my eyes. One by one, thankful to each as if he were a new being created for my use, I had heard their three voices . . . They were all beside me, bending over me . . . I felt their breath on my body, one touching my hand, another my cheek, the other my throat. All the rest of my body was icy; these three points boiling. Each one of their words, too, touched a precise fibre in me; a muscle of my leg, a point in my brain, and at times a part of me that

I had thought was spiritual and not sensual.   All
three voices as different as for an opera; the bass,
the baritone and tenor; and I vowed to open my
eyes as soon as all united in a trio phrase.   But each
spoke only in his turn.   English words, whose sense
I certainly understood, but which caused a movement in my memory that had no connection with
their content; and each word opened in me a vision
of Europe and drained it like a gland . . .

The bass voice was saying: "The feet baffle me.
Here is the thirty-first race to add to Wellney's
thirty races.   But the presence of cambered feet in
Polynesia is the ruin of Spencer and Heurteau!"

I understood all this, but how different were my
thoughts!

I was thinking of the arrival at stations! when
the train describes a tiny curve in order to enter the
shed; when the approach to Paris makes one so
sensitive that one can feel each switch beneath one.
The arrival at Saincaize, just at the exit of the tunnel, where they throw cherry stones on the travelers
leaving the train from Bourges!

The high voice said: "But that skin?"

"Painted and nacreous.   The skin is explained
in Wellney. But the feet confound me."

I was thinking: Wine, a bottle of which was there

perhaps, close by! The vine-stock on the hill-sides, wound around props, like beautiful hair-curlers on the eve before confirmation! The vintages, when the peaches are ripe and they open them and replace the pit by a muscat grape! . . .

The baritone voice asked: "Is it a maiden?"

"The most maidenly maiden in the world. Once passed Rimsky Island they tear off the right ear-lobe of those who are no longer virgins. At Salou they tattoo an open hand on the sole of the foot. But try and tattoo a hand on those feet there!"

Lemonade; soda-water, with saccharine! the flat bottle that is discovered in a cupboard a month after the passage of the little Elichades! Couzan water, Perier water, champagne!

"Abandoned in the island. All the young girls who are accused of divination are isolated for four years according to Wellney. Think of them tearing off the lobe at fifteen. At nine in Barre Island. This girl is twenty years old."

Chateaux, churches, canals, gardens, highways, roads, paths, foot-trails . . . mountain, snow, glaciers, foot-trails, paths, roads, highways, autos, the river at last, and the great bridge!

"But her skin, Billy."

"Painted and nacreous."

Billy was in such haste to reply that the high voice and the low voice were blended! . . .

Men; little ones, big ones, stutterers, deaf men, mustached ones, shaven ones; those in jackets, those whose hat flies off and is held by the broom of a sweeper . . . I had only to open my eyes in order to see all this . . . But the high voice was growing peevish . . .

"Painted and nacreous; that's all you know how to say. But underneath the paint?"

Dogs, cats; cages and aquariums watched over by cats, porcelain cats that sleep with golden spots and their names written below in pencil!

"Brown skin. Wellney type. I put a little acid on her arm. Look . . . "

Then something pricked me. With his finger he rubbed my arm in the hollow of my elbow. Between men and myself, by a biting acid, contact was reassumed forever . . . I opened my eyes . . . I saw all three of them.

"Jack, she is crying," said the high voice, "Console her."

Then Jack, the one who had already touched me (I had seen the mark of his hands on me) the one who was already acquainted with my body and who had carried me, the one who knew my weight, (I saw on his blue silk shirt a pearly trail like the one the moon leaves) and my perfume, approached, lifted my head; and at last I was able to speak and continue my conversation with men after so many years, to speak my first French word, which made Jack recoil stupefied and the other two approach: "A handkerchief!" I said.

.   .   .   .

Now it was the evening of the same day, and all four of us had stopped talking. My birds, astonished at seeing me remain in the second island, flew back to the first, almost flying backward. Each sunbeam quitted us also in order to rest for a moment on my true kingdom and go out. I was now clothed in black silk pyjamas; I now had a gold watch-chain for an anklet: I returned to European life by way of its most snobbish fashions. I returned to European tastes by way of their sharpest degree: rum, champagne, pickles. I was a little drunk; the earth again started to revolve for me.

By now I knew all about the war. I still hesitated, because of my friends' English accent, over the names of their Marshals, Pétain and Foch, but I knew all their adventures. Jack, who seemed to be the strategist, had insisted on showing me the Marne maneuver which had saved France:

flank right, then flank left. The Bouchavesne maneuver which saved the town hall of Bouchavesne:
flank left, then flank right. And finally the maneuver of one of his own patrols by which he had
captured two Uhlans, a marvellous combination of
the two preceding victories: flank left-right, then
flank right-left. From Hawkins, who was on the
staff, I had learned the gossip of all the armies:
Lady Abbley's visit disguised as a butcher boy; his
automobile trip with Clemenceau, from whom he
had admiringly awaited confidences and who merely
said to him after two days of silence, pointing out
some cows in a meadow: "If they fed cows coffee
they would give *café au lait*." And Lord Asquith's
stupor at seeing in the dining room, a year after
the beginning of the war, a full-length portrait of
Emperor William. As for Billy, he spoke little and
carried all his souvenirs on him: a fragment of a
grenade in his hand that hindered him from boxing
the compass and which had caused him to commit
great errors in navigation aboard the yacht; a service order, signed at once by an English general
named French and a French general named Lang-
lais. Then, as though he had been a billeting Lieutenant, he could tell me as fast as I furnished him
with Limousin names what English troops had

camped in various towns: the Hindus at Saint-Sulpice; the New Zealanders at Limoges; the Syrian
Jews at Rochechouart; and two Boer squadrons to
guard the Russian mutineers near Ussel. I also
learned the fashions for the year; they showed me
Vogue and *Feuillets d'art;* and, in order to prove to
me how much they esteemed me and how sure they
were that I belonged to their world, they enumerated
the latest marriages for me; unanimous in blaming
Priscilla Bandenby who married without love and
in yellow.

Now, thanks to this silk and these foulards, all
my tastes returned to me, more intractable than
ever. I had been seeing men again for barely twelve
hours, and, instead of giving complete approval to
them and to their creations, as I would have anticipated, I felt myself as intransigent as at boarding
school. Once more there were colors that I detested;
the violet of Hawkins' shirt, for example. I had no
pity for initialed cravats; I was irritated by shoes
that had over-large toe-caps; there was already a
champagne that I preferred. I obliged Billy to
change his socks, which were marked by concentric
stripes. I loved little pipes with short straight
stems, at the expense of pipes with curved stems.
I considered silvery blond hair and strong hands

worthy of our caresses as definitely as I
scorned black hair parted in the middle and little
supple hands. I would prefer platinum to gold,
Palmers to dry biscuits, Dearly mustard to ordinary
mustard. In one afternoon I had become mistress
of all those truths that a generation grasps in twenty
years. I, who had been weak with joy that very
morning at the thought of a trader or a merchant,
found it natural that my three saviours should be
young millionaire astronomers, come here at their
own expense to observe eclipses. I, who had wished
almost indifferently for the arrival of a Papuan, a
Chinaman or a negro, found that among these three
young lords—of whom the first was a duke, the
third a viscount—there was one who made the
presence of the others almost useless to me; by
chance the least titled, and the richest: an invincible
inclination carried me towards Jack.

I did not know how to contain myself. Every
time he got up it was difficult for me to keep from
following his steps like a dog. At times I saw all
three of my companions laugh: it was because (for
I kept the habit of thinking out loud for a long
time still) I had just uttered one of those phrases
in the infinitive that for me replaced reasoning. I
had just said: "To hold Jack in my arms!" "To

make him drink!" "To twist his identity bracelet until he cried!" This did not give Jack cause for pride and hardly even moved him: in the hospital he had had a trepanned man for his neighbor who talked the way I did. He cared for me as for the trepanned fellow: at each unconscious word of mine, he came up and wanted to push a new pillow under my head. Night had fallen. The launch chauffeur came for orders like an automobile chauffeur before the theatre in Paris. (To repair the bosom of the chauffeur's shirt, sewed on inside out! To tint green the white streak in the chauffeur's wig!) My friends stretched out, all three close to one another (To gently bump their three heads together!) and each one, after a certain number of billion stars, went to sleep. I was afraid; these three astronomers, extended and motionless, were strewing the island with new shadows that walked; but I did not dare awaken them: night is not an eclipse.

I could not go far from Jack. I had crawled towards him. In vain I was saying to myself everything that Mademoiselle had said to me: that for the first time in my life I was not a well bred young girl; that a well bred young girl does not hold a man's hand, does not kiss his forehead; that she does not cover the sloping chest of an astronomer-lieutenant with little pebbles, one by one, to attain the maximum weight at which respiration is checked. Beside this sleeping body, and for the first time moreover, I turned to account the craft and agility that I had gained in the island. I saw everything in spite of the night. Fearful lest a bird wake, I pricked this young man with a thorn to see him move, sigh. Without his perceiving it I replaced his cushions under his head. I laid siege to this sleeper. I made up his face, I painted his lips. Beside him I placed the herb that induces dreams. He clucked his tongue to excite a horse; he wiggled the third finger of his right hand: my Polynesian herb made him dream of a cart ride down Riverside. Having climbed into the manchineel just above his head I kept watch over him after the fashion of tigers who let themselves fall on the passerby. At the moment when his dream appeared to torment him, I let myself drop down beside him, driving away the dream without awakening him. Clad in pearl in this lunar debauch, like a sneak-thief clad in black in darkness, I ransacked his pockets, although a well bred young girl has orders not to do such things. With what joy I divided everything with him, each tree, each bird in this world which yesterday had still been so terribly indivisible! But how he was sleeping! Already however, the parrots—which thanks to him were no longer any more than my half-parrots —the sparrows—my half-sparrows—were commencing to circle round and round. My thousand half-stars moved gently, my half-Pacific no longer quite filled the horizon; it was the hour when the world is set in motion; it is morning. The saw on the reefs grated as at the end of a log. Stretched out at last, but as ill at ease on the soil of this new island on which I had never slept as on a new bed, I impatiently waited: I had forgotten to ask them the season. I awaited their awakening in order to know whether it were spring or summer. And at last (I did not wait for his part) my half-sun appeared!

Then I threw myself on Jack and laughingly shook him; I succeeded in doing with his body just the opposite to what I had done with the seventeen bodies of the past year; I pulled him by the arms and the hair down to the lagoon; I flung him, covered with dew, into the fresh water in which only the night fish were moving as yet. His comrades were laughing, awakened by his cries; and, united by that thread which links friends and Alpine climbers, they leaped in after us.

.   .   .   .

17

What more is there to tell you? It was at the moment that Billy announced breakfast to me that I felt the same feeling for him as for Jack. The same desire to touch him, to kiss him. The same love for his parents and his family, the same inexhaustible sympathy for his slightest movement, the same devotion to his virtues. I stifled under my hand words that all three still believed were avowals to Jack but which were hymns to Billy. It was toward Billy, my back to Jack, that I turned during the siesta. I set myself to attack his daytime sleep as I had Jack's nocturnal sleep. With the same thorn, with the same caress; without seeing his face this time, despite the sun, for he had covered it with a handkerchief. But I truly experienced the same desire—felt with Jack during the night—that Billy should have a sister, a house. Exactly the same wish to travel at his side; to see Billy silhouetted against a flaming volcano; to see, Billy's hand in my hand, young crocodiles descending the Ganges, their snouts imperceptibly turning toward the fattest child among each group of pilgrims. Jack had awakened behind me; he was teasing me with a palm leaf, like a man who believes that he is still loved; and, turning around at last, I perceived with astonishment, moreover, that he still was. My thought, despite my passion for Billy, did not despoil Jack of all those charms with which I had laden him at every stage of his body like a Christmas tree. I loved Billy and Jack. What, indeed, might all this signify? Either Providence was regulating things too well and was delivering me by means of the only two men in the world who could please me; or my heart, grown rusty for five years, was no longer anything but a mill.

But what was I to think that evening when Hawkins modestly, for he saw that the others were preferred, asked me to listen to the phonograph. As he was turning the needle and resting his hand on the record, closing his eyes so that his finger might better feel the markings; as he was starting to sit down afterwards, and hesitating, finding only places (apart from cactus bushes) which were ornamented with pearl-shells, orchids and coral, and none for which man was an ornament; halting with embarrassment for a moment, for Jack and Billy had chosen the *Marseillaise* and had to stand up to hear it,—just then a tic of Hawkins's eyebrows threw this friend, alive, into my heart. It was a still stronger love than for the others, since more distant members of his family were touched by it. To visit Hawkins' grandfather one day when the snow is falling on

London, giving to England the sole resemblance
that it can have to my pearly shore! To swim
in the Ganges with the grandson of Hawkins's
sister, beside great boats with moving birds in
their immobile rigging, with sleeping fish in their
wake! To go to Compiègne by auto with Hawkins's
first-cousin; to be afraid because he drives with
his eyes fixed on me! Hawkins now was again
looking for a place to sit down, for the music
had finished with national anthems. The phonograph was playing *Sous les ponts de Paris*.
Hawkins made me explain the French words to him,
and then sang the refrain, chewing the tune of these
words which were new to him as though with new
teeth. Then it was a tango, and I was astonished to
read on his face, down to the least details, all that a
tango can suggest to the mind of an Oxford student.
Five years of solitude had taught me to divine from
twitching lips or the reflections on cheeks what
proper names or city names were crossing a man's
thought . . . Besides, there was nothing illogical in
Hawkins's reverie. In that first second he was
dreaming of Havana: he saw a transhipping passenger who wildly watched his hat-trunk fall into the
sea. In that second second,—of two statues in the
harbor of Bahia, whose ears are gigantic shells,—

one, too, was false and it was impossible to listen to the sea through it. In that second,—of Madrid, of the squint-eyed cashier at the Palace Hotel, of Goya, of Velasquez. Then suddenly, the tango finished,— of nothing very much; of nothing . . . How I loved him!

And night returned. The phonograph, the electric lamp of the launch through the cocoanut trees, the cry of a distant monkey,—all these troubled my soul as the disturbances of a suburban public garden, and before a mirror I could have divined from my face some terrible words that were passing through me and rending me utterly: *Vesinet, La Garenne-Bezons,* perhaps *Bois-Colombes* . . . On the shore the mechanician was whistling tunes already played, but two or three records behind. I knew that he was busy combining all the blue, white and red things in the wardrobe in order to put a French flag at the stern; but I hesitated to go to see him: I was not sure that I did not love him! He came at last, offering me the flag, puffed up on his two hands like swaddling-clothes containing a baby. He had that assured speech, those square-irised eyes, that waddling of the shoulders which, combined with bright blue and yellow cravats, make chauffeur-mechanicians dearer to you than love.

.   .   .   .

Billy, who was only an antelope hunter and who detested astronomy, had thought of taking me to the yacht, anchored off Rimsky-Korsakoff, in the desire, I believe, of showing me his collection of skins and antlers the following day; but I decided to leave only with all of them and to wait for the eclipse. They approved my decision, for they feared that the eclipse would be accompanied by a typhoon; and I had plenty of time to present my island to them. It was ready . . . At bottom, the anxiety for this reception had guided all my acts for five years. I had made the island a park, a drawing-room; shining the beaches with pearl, polishing the reefs, coloring whole bushes vivid red by injections in their roots, and bordering them afterward with black orchids; wiping from the marine caves that dust which the Ocean gives as plentifully as a Provence road. I had, too, disdained encumbering my island with objects which might be useful but which would be ridiculous the day I was saved: tables, chairs or tubs. It was a garden without a newspaper on the lawn, without a dead leaf; in fine, the best waxed island in Polynesia; and Billy slipped on the coral. I had trained the very birds in the ways of an aviary; always feeding them on the same rings, relegating the garden-nests of the gardner-birds to a single

meadow which was quite covered with their workman's houses; stripping the moss (my trees' one
ugliness) from the mangroves so that they might not
be surprised in this flannel; and stretching along the
alleys my feather curtains (exactly like the curtains
with which they camouflage roads near the front, said
Hawkins, with the difference that mine were of paradise feathers). The reception was belated, the shrubs
had become trees, the parrots spoke a human language; but this hour when tea was served in four
coconut cups seemed to justify in the eyes of God
—and in any case justified in my eyes—five years of
drama and misfortune.

Then the eclipse took place, augmenting Billy's
irritation, for he could not comprehend the emotion
of the two astronomers and failed to understand in
what way terrestial phenomena are excelled by solar
and lunar. He fumed, while we three remained
silent because of this veil thrown over the moon, as
canaries do when their cage is covered. He compared each of the stars to some animals that he had
hunted and did not succeed in arriving at a preference. He inveighed against all those instruments that
Hawkins and Jack aimed at the sky without ever
firing; then he was suddenly appeased and non-
plussed by a shooting star, for they touched his

heart.   He disappeared, and I perceived him later
carving words on the rock of the headland with a
blow-torch.   He looked like a burglar forcing the
secrets of the island; in fact, he was adding one to
them.   He was writing:

THIS ISLAND IS SUZANNE ISLAND
WHERE POLYNESIAN DEMONS
TERRORS
EGOTISM
WERE CONQUERED BY A YOUNG GIRL
FROM BELLAC

The launch left the following day, heading into
the sun.   No typhoon.   The sea was peaceably calm
as one who has renounced an anger.   I was seated
facing my island.   Little by little it grew round;
for the first time I saw it from a slight distance, from
afar off, from the horizon.   It was sparkling; it was
now no more than rubies and topazes; all those rays
in which I had been caught for six years now touched
me only at their apex, my head alone was still lighted
by them; a mile more and I would again assume my
dull European light, under the real rice powder which
Hawkins had loaned me.   But above all my island
seemed inhabited.   In the fronds in the shapes of
the hills, there was—brought by me alone—that

harmony which forty million Frenchmen have just
succeeded in imposing on their mountains and their
forests. My island had been made use of exactly
like France. Above it, in numberless and regular
flights which ended in a human being, like the trail
of a comet, there flew birds; whereas they are more
scattered above other islands than bubbles in Saint-
Glamier water. At times a tree which I had always
believed co-mingled with the others appeared alone
to me and bid me an individual farewell. The places
that I had believed were my surest hiding-places
were also apparent for the most part: it was when
I had wept or prayed that I had been most visible.
Then the second island approached mine, slipped it a
reflection that it accepted and hid, as a woman, who
is taking her friend to the train, does with the note
of the friend who remains behind. Then the launch
was jarred: it was the last ressaut of the swell
against my reefs. Then a contraction of my heart:
it was, doubtless, the line at which the Kanakas, torn
from their native land, fling themselves into the sea.
Two or three of my favorite birds accompanied me
for a long time; then, at some farther boundary,
heart-broken but constrained, they abandoned me. I
was crying. Billy for the first time damned the land,
and turned me forcibly toward the bow just at the

second when my island disappeared, as one turns a child's head at the exact moment when the gentleman in the bed dies.

Thus I quitted my island. At times I shivered, believing I had been grazed afresh by one of my birds; but it was the wind which was carrying away one of the thousand paradise remnants heaped up on the deck. With eyes as swollen with tears as a boarding-school girl entering a convent, I watched the little trunk that my friends had loaned me sliding about. Little boarding-school trousseau that contained only litres of pearls . . . Billy tried to distract me by talking to me about Wilson, Victor Hugo, and Verlaine, as they had talked to me, when I was a little girl, about the teachers and under-teachers that I was going to have in Europe . . . Hawkins who had the best view of all and who was turned toward the stern, remained so for a half-hour with an opera glass. Then he took my hand and said suddenly: "It's all over: it can be seen no more . . ."

So it was that my island became invisible . . .

What is there to tell you now?

How, the same evening I caught sight of another land, then another with hills, then another with mountains, and felt as if the sea, the deluge, were subsiding? How Billy (nothing in me, doubtless, being solar or lunar) became amorous in his turn and would not let me go? How my rescue landed me at the most distant point from France that a Frenchwoman can reach? Farther from France, said Jack, there was only Lelestra, the nearest star. How, because of a tidal wave, warned by our wireless, we put into another uninhabited island for two days? . . . At bottom, escape had spoiled me; here the fruit was more bitter, the coconuts harder to break . . . How I again got used to sleeping in a bed; first on the floor in front of the bed; then on the carpet; then on cushions; regaining sleep by degrees, as a favorite regains the throne? How Billy cried each evening at nine o'clock—for he was as exact as a watch—when I refused his hand? We were stretched out in hammocks on the bridge. Big stars hung down to us and then suddenly pulled themselves up; but we would not play at this stupid game. We played lotto, the only game on board. Already the stars and the birds were once more becoming alien molecules for me . . . Many times the yacht tried to announce by radio that I had been found, but the apparatus lacked power, and only some brave planters and recruiting officers, isolated for six months in the archipelagos, could rejoice at the news. Sometimes an overturned ship's boat: it was a Kanaka deserter from a ship, I was told, who must have been caught in the sandbank beneath. Then, one day, a schooner, whose old captain started to dance around in a ring when he learned of my rescue. His cargo was whiskey and Bordeaux and he signalled us that he was going to give me a celebration.

"Marry me," said Billy. "You love me!"

"No, Billy."

"Marry me," repeated Billy, who tempted me with all the proper names that signify luxury and beauty: "We will have a Kauderlen yacht, the complete service of the vessel will be of Keller silver. What a fine noise in the tempests! You love me!"

But I loved everyone. My solitude had raised the pitch of that vague indifference that we feel for our fellow-men, and it began at love. In all of Lewis Island I tried to find one human being that I could not love . . . But to contemplate for five minutes the iris of a pearl fisher, which had become microscopic because of diving; the malice in the eye-ball of a bishop; the faith in a God more beautiful than the most beautiful Kanaka, in the pupil of a Kanaka, and not to feel oneself transported with love by them! The approach of every human being intoxicated me like a pipe of opium. I restrained myself from kissing them and breathing their breath, their sparkling eyes. I stopped before each human head as before a cage and whistled to birds. Even on Rateau Island—where the people live greedily dividing the air with breaths, collecting their eyes, nose and mouth all at the top of their heads like parasites, as if they were going to dive and rid their heads of them, little by little, by staying under—I could not find one who horrified me. Not even in Papua . . . That dawn on the banks of the Fly! Everything was asleep, save for some little wading-birds that were walking on the lily-pads without submerging them . . . A great moon-bow rose with the seven colors of the rainbow (shall I recite them for you) plus a golden one. A cassowary squatting beside me shot his still blind head into the air like an elastic, withdrawing the white skin from his eyes and, seeing me, fled away on great feet that had brought his ancestors from island to island after leaving Tasmania. Jeannot the Kanaka, whom we named "Republic" because he had been condemned to death, and reprieved, at Noumea for insulting the Republic —we held him by this word; the least wanton insult and his sentence would again be effective!—Jeannot was going to bathe, leaving behind him, as he shook the creepers of jasmine, a more perfumed trail than

the head-salesman at Guerlain's,* and sending you
later by his diving a whiff of hot wine and cinnamon
that was the odor of the Fly.   Finally Dr. Albertino
appeared, followed by the wives of a Papuan chief
who sold him rare insects for twenty francs (how
dear life was getting!).   He had a large black beard
through which there sometimes appeared a little
white gesticulating hand,—his own.   In the evening,
at the village celebration, in order to make the
Papuans retain their faith in sorcery, he burned a
little, a very little, with his alcohol (he hoarded it
for pickling his new snakes) and swallowed flames.
He had little outfits of white alpaca, executed, he
said, by M. Tomasi, the one tailor in the world who
was not bothered by the problem of suspenders.

It was on July 1st, 1918, that we arrived at
Honolulu, where the bishop's daughter, learning that
I had no dress, sent me one of the most beautiful
among her own, and—chance or Hawaiian custom—
came to await me at the palace in a twin dress.   She
was the first dressed woman I had seen; I threw
myself into her arms; for an instant we were but one
form in green silk.   From the yacht, Billy with his
spy-glass might have thought that one does not re-
store a woman to her sex with impunity and that I

* Parisian perfumer.

had melted into it at first meeting. We had to leave at the end of an hour: never had the Hawaiian choir had to sing, with so brief an interval between, the hymn of the maiden who comes and the hymn of the maiden who goes.

In New York, M. Cazenave gave a dinner at Sherry's in my honor. There were present, in brief, a French commander who had an iron hand, and a lieutenant who had a mechanical gauntlet; and the first French flesh that I could grasp was a horrid metal. The captain had a silver plate in his skull; I rediscovered my compatriots as though after a boiler explosion. When I asked a fourth, a little farther off, how many officers were in their mission, he raised his hand, spreading it to show me there were five, forgetting that he now had only four fingers. But the war had spared in each of them exactly the feature by which he could please me; and it made me happy to think that I loved the least perishable part in men. I was the only person in the world who had not yet heard war stories: you can imagine if they profited by the fact. The command-ant, a little familiar, occasionally touched me with his iron hook, as though to stir, without destroying, a beautiful fire. Happier than if they were reveal-ing to the Sleeping Beauty after her awakening the invention of powder, printing, truffles, and champagne, they explained trenches, barbed wire, and *sacs barbelés,* smiling to themselves at the word "cavalry." It was at this moment, quite by chance, that my eyes came to rest on Edward Marion, my vis-à-vis . . . My glance passed over this face at first distractedly; and I could not understand the pain that I experienced. A moment later, the same anguish of heart, and I remembered having looked at Marion for a second time . . . Then five times, ten times, I repeated the experiment . . . and I understood . . . I actually had before me the first man in whom I found nothing to love . . .

The dinner, however, had reached that stage at which everyone discovers himself and loves himself in his neighbour. M. Cazenave discovered a cousin of his brother-in-law's in a young Irishwoman, embraced her, discovered Ireland. Miss Pond was discovering that Sargent is a great poet and Hugo a great painter. Mrs. Dallmore found two measures from Beethoven in The Star Spangled Banner. Mr. Hoover, taken in hand by one of our propagandists, was discovering that Algeria and Tunisia are French colonies, and was in raptures . . . But I expended all my glances on Edwin's head. However, in less than a minute he made all those gestures by which

character is revealed. In one moment I saw him
laugh, speak, drink, eat, hiccough, and pick his teeth,
ears and finger nails. One would have said that his
sole occupation was to free himself from the alluvium
with which he was covered afresh each second. I
saw him inattentive, dejected, gay, overflowing with
health and undermining a table-leg with his two
knees; raising his hand to his forehead, ill . . . On
his half-breed American face, where each ancestral
feature successively dominated the others, I saw
Scotchman, Jew, Hollander, Bostonian. I saw him
—for he had odd eyes and hair of different colors, as
though there were to his head a north and a south
side—red-haired with a blue eye or salt-gray with a
dark eye, according to the profile that he offered me.
I saw him hypocritically slide his hand forward in order to surprise his glass. I saw him
seize a fringe of the table-cloth and tear it little
by little. He threw his bread under the table;
then, the alluvium disposed of once more, he washed
his chin and fingers with moistened handkerchief.
M. Cazanave, who was amused at my revulsion, told
me that everyone found Edwin antipathetic as I did,
but that he was a man of genius, that his drawings
and captions were celebrated, that no throne could
resist his caricatures; and, moreover, that when he
18

became too arrogant it was only necessary to speak
to him of death. He shut up immediately; he took
flight, like a couguar that is shown a match.

Edwin had now closed his eyes. He enjoyed the
privilege of falling asleep as soon as he wished. He
had slipped down in his chair, his beard thrust forward. He was sleeping with a cloth surcharged with
twenty women, silver, flowers and liquors for a
sheet, and his finger marks were visible on it, for
they marked like his charcoal. At times a wink or
start made one guess that one of his future captions,
one of his future sarcasms, was traveling through
him like a needle through a child's body . . . and it
suddenly grazed a vital organ (the liver, for he
turned completely yellow) and awakened him . . .

He now observed me with a suspicious eye, as if
he understood that I had learned about him during
his nap. From time to time, whenever the conversation turned toward the sea and ships or away
from it, the guests turned toward him to praise
his already celebrated drawing, showing a ship in a
tempest, which had appeared in the *Sun* the evening
before, and the whole table smiled at him admiringly.
He suddenly spoke to me, complimenting me upon
having been discovered in my island. I was determined to locate by speech, that weak and sympathetic

spot in him that no glance had been able to find.   I
smiled at him . . .

"And you," I said, "who will ever discover you in
yours? . . ."

"I am discovered," he replied.   "I have a besotted
wife and three idiot children."

I could not respond, for M. Vinocht was extolling
a famous edition of Coleridge's *Tempest,* and all
around him were profiting by this to turn and bow
toward Edwin.   A plastered lady continued to nod
her head like a Chinese tumbling-toy, until Edwin
stopped her with a grimace.   He told me that she
derived her income from the most beautiful cemetery
in Saint Louis, selling the most expensive places, for
it was in the center of a public garden.   It was even
said that she got away with her boarders' gold
teeth . . .

"That's a cemetery you should avoid," said I.

For he had three gold teeth.   He looked at me
mistrustfully, asking himself if I had not been forewarned of his phobia; thereafter he watched my
slightest movement, awaiting my least word, like a
man who knows another's revolver is loaded; offering me asparagus with oil, speaking ill of the white
sauce to me with all the baseness of someone who is
afraid of a spectre; betraying the most beautiful

woman in the party to me by recounting her passion
for her chauffeur; employing more villanies to avoid
the mere word "death" and to distract me than most
people would employ to elude death itself; resorting
to tricks which might make me believe in his frankness in order to win me; speaking well of Germany
to me, ill of France,—and he was thinking of neither
one nor the other.   I spoke to him of Daumier, who
was dead, of Degas, who had just died; but he
questioned me regarding Vuillard, Bonnard, and all
those who had a long time to live (like one who
replaces real cartridges by false ones in the revolver
on the table) pretending, until I insisted other-
wise, to believe that Degas was still living; senile,
but living; in a coma, but living . . .

Yonder the orchestra was playing *le Vaisseau fan-
tome,* and everyone smiled at him again and bowed
toward him. . . .   I abandoned the project. . . .
Sight, smell, hearing had been exhausted in vain;
he could not have nobility or worthiness in him, save
some metal entered by chance: a swallowed *louis
d'or,* a silver pharynx . . .   Perhaps touch would
indicate it to me yet. . . .   As he advanced his fingers toward a carafe, I brushed his hand by a
studiedly clumsy gesture: it was cold, smooth,
hard.   He looked at me, the same insincere expres-

sion in his eyes, guessing what I was going to say, already thrusting aside his napkin, almost standing up. . . . I said to him. . . . "You have the hands of death. . . ."

He saluted me, to turn aside some witch-craft, and fled. . . .

Then I turned toward the others, and suddenly I saw that they, too, in consequence of this unclean power, had been withdrawn from my heart. Edwin, in order to flee, had unhooked that chain by which each person had fastened my glance to one of his features or his movements. They were there, before me, evidently successful in their fashion, like little patés done to a turn: a little more cooking and Madame Blumenoll's rouge and Mrs. Baldwann's heart would melt. Some remained sympathetic, emerging above the others; I fished them out again as I had formerly done with my bits of wreckage. I looked at Billy: I saw a big pink and white child, good, handsome, witty, rich, and kind,—a poor child! He smiled at me, he, the millionaire, who was thinking at this moment of our golden Pic-Pic automobile, our silvery Plumet villa, our bediamond Rolls Royce existence. But I closed my eyes . . . I had lost Billy, too. . . . Across the way they were talking about the Lusitania, and all turned towards

Edwin's place with flattering smiles, astonished at finding it empty.

Now I was on the terrace of the Plaza. Stretched out in a cubby-hole fourteen stories above me, Billy, poor human bottle, warned of my decision, was weeping. I saw great luminous lines cut the city in four parts like a cake, some cutting down to the macadam, others yonder pressed lightly; one would have to pull yonder to tear away that part, which would come with shreds of flooring covered with sleeping children and couples. . . . I saw the shadows of trees entrust themselves to the trees or fly from them with all their strength, depending on the gas lamps. I saw the great wheels and Broadway signs turn according to astral laws. Never was the Milky Way more brutally reflected than it was by Broadway that evening. Even in that night, even in that tranquillity, I felt that I had failed in the power, loaned me by God, of seeing in each human being the gift which renders him superior to all others; and animals, and objects themselves, fell back for me into their common lot, which is to please or displease. And among those flying bats, only one, who passed by and returned, pleased me; and among those night watchmen, a circle of light around each of them, that moved about in the darkness like islands, only one, who stopped every time I counted ten, excited my love, my suffering. Champagne enervated me, too, and, like the terrace piled with people—a fat financier and his wife, a snob and his fiancée, two sisters, two brothers—my thought, which had been so straight and pure all day long, was lost in these couples, ending in the night through them as through a delta . . . With a thousand winkings the stars were recruiting for eternity. . . . The wind was blowing on them, on me, and on the perishable cedars . . . Like a man who wishes to commit suicide at Niagara Falls, and who, suddenly modest, having returned to his hotel, drowns himself in the bathtub, so I, confused suddenly by the royal solitude of my island, gave myself up until morning to those two poor square metres of solitude in the midst of seven million men. . . .

.   .   .   .

I have just crossed the Atlantic, innocent of coral and sharks. Near Europe, a dirigible threw down to the yacht newspapers full of photographs. The armistice had just been signed by Lloyd George who looks like a poodle, by Wilson who looks like a collie, and by Clemenceau who looks like a housedog. Europe had the highest hopes for this peace signed by men who resemble dogs.

It is still night.   But I wished to have the yacht put me off alone, at random, and leave me as soon as the first French land was sighted.   Billy accompanied me in the same automobile launch that had taken me from my island.   Through pines and shadows I heard the noise of the same motor that had awakened me among palms and coral.   Billy had wished to equip me with a litre of gin, a cake, and a Manilla shawl.   I had refused all this foreign paraphenalia.   I was thirsty, cold, and hungry, too.

Now I am waiting, as on the morning of my shipwreck, standing up then sitting down, on this France that is going to swallow me up before morning.   As yet I can recognize none of it.   Billy told me that La Rochelle must be close by; but in vain I remain alert for one of those noises or signs that a prefecture ought to give toward midnight.   Only the ocean makes big and little disturbances of so particular a kind that I recognize them as Saintongeian.   Only the sky has a known form, which I put on as the one hat which suits me after six years.   I am penetrated only by that assurance of equilibrium which one feels in caressing the earth, the grain of one's country, with one's hand.   Silence alone has that sonority of my childhood which suddenly gives me all nature and the night for ears.   But those gestures which I had anticipated (and even rehearsed in my cabin) for the trees and birds of France, those trees that I will climb no more; that restraint, too, face to face with old leaves, and ephemeral flowers; that modesty with forests and flower-beds,—all these are devoid of object so far.   Through the darkness I perceive only pines similar to those on the island; the perfume that I breathe is that of magnolias, as it was yonder; and my hand that slips into the first bush—that I think is alder or maple—more tenderly than into a person's hair, encounters only spindle-tree or fern.   In my absence my country must have grown old and hard, renouncing species with mortal leaves, no longer entrusting its flora to the hazards of spring. . . .   No matter; I entrust myself to the hazards of day!

But now the owl flies softly around me   Now the shrew-mouse, chased by it, utters its cry.   Now a breath, a light wind that had never brushed me save when I returned by carriage, the bride in bed at last, from the Dorat or Bessines wedding.   Now it forces me to turn my face toward it.   Now I am replaced, oriented by it, in one of the night-watches of France.   Here is the invariable order that carries me like a rolling sidewalk; a wailing chaffinch, yonder the song of the cock.   Behold my night located on my chart; I now know its exact depth. I am in that short watch when the nightingale is stilled, and rests before his last song. It is indeed he who flutters beside me, who brushes modest me, as a *lieder* singer who dominates the scene brushes against a supernumerary; and now it is the last watch of the nightingale. Never has nightingale sung nearer me. His throat swells. As at the movies, when one sits too near the screen, I am within these waves of misery, of happiness, issuing from a nightingale; I shiver. Comes the three-forty-five wind, the four o'clock sound of bells. Beside me the ocean is milky, at once humble, hypocritical and content: having, doubtless, just been filled by a new million drowned. But suddenly a trumpet yonder has sounded reveillé. Toward the four points of the compass it sounds. To all twenty-year-old Frenchmen stretched out toward the South, West, and North it announces that the sun is going to rise. At this moment it sounds to the East. The whole mouth of the trumpet must be golden.

Now the dawn, and that cold which the first ray brings. It is surely France, despite this last false decoration of magnolias and of pines. From the largest of these trees escapes a magpie, like a French word it can no longer restrain. Now two magpies, three, four; now a green woodpecker, now starlings, now entire phrases. It is indeed the coast at which my country's rivers end, and I shiver at their estuary like a young salmon. Beside this field of hares, I am actually breathing the light mist which allures the poachers and that half-light that allures the police. I hear indeed, as on our farms, the watching animals exchange their cries for a moment: the dog hoot, the owl bay. Behold, I come to you oh France, without a valise, but with a body prepared for you; with hunger and with thirst; a body starved for your wine and your omelette,—and now comes the rising sun! I recognize you France, from the size of your wasps, your mulberries, your cock-chafers, and— what happiness to have escaped from that dream which gave me power over birds—the birds fly from me! A move towards the nightingale, and—oh happiness!—he flies! Carts are grating. For the first time in six years I am set in motion at dawn like other creatures, by gravitation, weight, work. A thresher is beating. For the first time I do not feel that I am the sole useless person in a universe on which, dear pumice stone, no other human being is sharpening his life. A train whistles. What joy not to be alone in France! I venture looking at it over the down. It is really a train . . . Behold

the cow which renders milk-trees useless, the vine
which renders the wine-tree useless. Behold yonder
the sheep that makes the wool-tree seem so paltry.
Crows feed on the northern edge of the field; magpies on the southern edge. From La Rochelle, still
invisible, I hear noises. The trumpet now sounds
the call for corporals and quarter-masters; life com-
mences in France for Frenchmen of these ranks.
Then the call for company commanders: life has
commenced for the middle-class. A gigantic rustling of silk and velvet: the middle-class is putting
on its uniform. Magistrates open their mail. Their
wives awake, languid with pride, and through half-
open windows there comes to them the noise of
trams and anvils. Ah! at this very name of
magistrate, of mortgage-officer, of registrar, my
title of Frenchwoman comes back to me like a
trade.

But I hear steps. I retain that Polynesian reflex
which compels you, when you hear steps, to climb
to the top of a cedar or to dive to the bottom of the
waters. I hide myself in a hollow tree. I hear a
voice. I retain that Polynesian desire which impels
you, to honor the words of the arrival, to repeat
them by singing at the top of your lungs. But it is
he himself who is singing. I see him. That first

tune that Hawkins played me on his phonograph
with wax and a needle, he sings with his finger on
his heart.

He arrives. . . . Here, then, this Frenchman,
who makes the hug-tree useless! Here is one
of those Frenchmen celebrated throughout the entire world for crossing populous streets and life
sideways, and without accident! I see him. I see
him as you do not know how to see, for I have not
regained the habit of separating in my thought what
I see that is physical from what I see that is moral.
He has two large mustaches and a limitless devotion.
He has a palpitating Adam's apple with a great need
for confidences. He has a sheathed scarf-pin with
a sweet obstinacy. . . . He does not leap up the
tree; he does not run into the water. He sticks to
earth like a light vase that one has put on the sand
to make a stable lamp. His feet scarcely leave the
ground, fanned by his coat; and his face illumines
at the same height bushes and animals. Here is the
Frenchman who replaces the lamp-tree for humanity. He is going to pass by without discovering me.
I cough, between the chorus and the couplet, for I
know that neither birds nor men hear when they
are singing. He turns back. He sees me come out
of my tree. The son of Latins and of Gauls he still

has those reflexes of people who see a dryad. He takes off his hat and strokes his mustache. He approaches little by little. He has two beautiful gray eyes and a love for stamp collections. He draws a glove from the pocket of his coat. He says to me:

"I am the Controller of Weights and Measures, Mademoiselle. . . . Why weep?"

FINIS